Goose on the Run

"And finally," the newscaster said, "a goose brought traffic to a standstill on the M3 motorway today. An eight-mile tailback of vehicles was unable to proceed, due to a young Canada goose with an injured wing. The goose successfully dodged cars and lorries as it headed for the central reservation, where it rested before losing itself among the traffic. Police contacted experts from a wild-fowl sanctuary, where it is believed to have resided, but all attempts to capture it have, so far, failed. A further update on the 'goose on the run' will be given on the nine o'clock news."

HIPPO ANIMAL

Goose on the Run

Brenda Jobling

Hippo

Dedicated to Ron, Rosemary and Jean

Scholastic Children's Books,
Commonwealth House, 1–19 New Oxford Street,
London WC1A 1NU, UK
a division of Scholastic Ltd
London ~ New York ~ Toronto ~ Sydney ~ Auckland

First published by Scholastic Ltd, 1997

Text copyright © Brenda Jobling, 1997

ISBN 0 590 19368 6

Typeset by TW Typesetting, Midsomer Norton, Somerset
Printed by Cox & Wyman Ltd, Reading, Berks.

10 9 8 7 6 5 4 3 2 1

Chapter 1

Above an early morning mist the sun shone like a great silver button in a pale sky. A young goose, its wings outstretched, struck out to fly further afield than it had ever flown before. The feathers on its long, proud neck and its powerful wings were tinged silver where the sun's rays touched them. The adventurous young goose flew swiftly and confidently through the air, not as one of a pair or in formation with other geese – but alone.

On the ground a ten-year-old boy named Josh sat huddled close to his uncle Charlie on the bank of a pond. The boy's uncle held a fishing-rod in his hands and both he and the boy were intent on watching for movement on the end of the line, which they could just see through the mist hovering over the surface of the water. The boy felt excited and slightly scared; the place had a sense of eeriness about it, like a prehistoric landscape. The sound of creatures moving and feeding on the water reached his ears, but the mist shrouded any sight of them.

For an instant Josh took his gaze from the line to look at the expression on his uncle's face. He loved the familiar profile of the favourite relative he also considered to be his best friend. Now that Uncle Charlie had taken early retirement from work, Josh anticipated even more fishing trips. Uncle Charlie's mouth had turned up, ever so slightly, at the corners, and Josh knew that to be a good sign. His uncle sensed the presence of the very special fish they sought. It had evaded them on many occasions and now it was extremely close to the line. Josh was aware he had to stay perfectly still and silent.

Just below the surface of the water lingered a

pale, golden Mirror Carp: a beautiful, chubby, shimmering fish. That morning Uncle Charlie felt certain the carp would surrender to them, just long enough to be weighed and photographed to provide evidence which would amaze and, no doubt, cause envy among other anglers who also sought to land the prized carp.

Less than a mile away, still high in the air, the young goose flew on through the brightening sky. Despite possessing strong wings, it began to tire. The goose had never flown so far from its home before. Now the need to rest, before a return journey, was its greatest desire. The goose decided to fly a little further and land, if possible, when it sensed water below.

At the side of the pond Uncle Charlie and Josh beamed with self-satisfied smiles. A vibration on the end of the line had travelled up the rod to Uncle Charlie's hands – the carp was interested in the bait. Uncle Charlie put a finger to his lips. Josh hardly dared breathe. There! They saw the float dip in the water. At any second, the bait could be taken.

Josh peered through the mist at the brightly-coloured float. He felt his heart pounding with excitement.

High above them the goose knew it would soon need to land, or be forced out of the sky by exhaustion. The powerful young wings had served it well, but it had overestimated its ability to fly so far from home. With relief, it sensed water below and immediately dropped height to prepare for landing upon the surface.

Uncle Charlie and Josh sat poised for action, aware of nothing but the sensation of the fish – it had to be the carp – nibbling tentatively at the bait. Josh was ready to grab the landing-net the moment his uncle started to reel in.

"Come *on*, my beauty! You *know* it tastes good," Uncle Charlie whispered, willing the fish to take the baited hook. There it was again! Definite movement on the line. The wily carp was playing with the bait. The fish made a worthy challenge for Josh and his uncle. Both of them itched to reel him in, but they knew patience would bring its own reward. The moment had to be exactly right: too soon, and the carp could be frightened off; too late, and the fish might lose interest, or become suspicious.

Below the water the carp had decided the sweet-tasting bait was too good to resist. His sensitive lips quivered around the mixture, the hook hidden deep at its centre.

In the sky above, oblivious of the silent battle raging below, the goose was losing height. As the ground seemed to rise up to meet it, the creature could see through the mist that the water on which it was forced to land wasn't a big expanse like the lake at home. Descending fast, all of its instincts were aroused to prepare it for a sudden landing. At the last moment, swerving through the trees like an out-of-control missile, the goose headed into the water.

At that very same moment in time, the carp's pale, rubbery mouth opened wide to take the

sweet bait, hook and all. But the sound of the goose landing with a loud thud and splash, only a few feet away in the reeds, sent the fish on its way. Uncle Charlie and Josh both experienced a sinking feeling deep in the pits of their stomachs as the carp rejected the bait. Before the goose had even hit the water, its shadow passing overhead had been enough to warn the fish off.

Frantically, Uncle Charlie reeled in the line, even though he knew his action was in vain. Josh and his uncle watched for a moment, as the beautiful, shimmering carp showed its back on the surface – flaunting itself – before moving off across the pond. Uncle Charlie stood motionless, staring at the ripples left by the departing fish. Josh, however, decided he should investigate the cause of the loud splash. He was sorry they had lost the carp – his uncle would be inconsolable for some time – but what about the thing that had fallen from the sky into the water? Josh was a little afraid, but his curiosity was stronger than his fear, and he was eager for an answer.

Before he went to investigate, he whispered

to his uncle, "Do you think it's a UFO? They always seem to land in quiet, misty places, and there's *always* just two people around to witness it."

As far as Josh's uncle was concerned, aliens may well have landed; it mattered little to him. He still stared, with a vacant expression, into the misty water. Slowly, he removed the old cap he always wore when fishing, ran his fingers through his damp hair, and let out a heavy sigh of disappointment. Josh thought his uncle didn't seem to be hearing him, so he continued, "*I'm* going to take a look."

The boy crept away in the direction of frenzied splashing. It was coming from a thick clump of reeds, a little way off. A few seconds later he felt himself dragged backwards by his collar in the firm grip of Uncle Charlie. Despite his misery at losing the carp, Josh's words had penetrated his thoughts and alerted him to the fact that his nephew could be heading into danger.

"Don't go off without me, Josh. I'd never forgive myself if I lost *you* as well as the carp!"

Uncle Charlie moved with care, positioning

himself in front of his nephew, to protect him. Armed with a stout stick he had picked up, he cautioned, "Shh! Hear that?" The boy and his uncle froze on the spot, like statues. They could hear the sound of reeds being beaten. The pair moved on, making slow progress, until they neared the narrow band of reeds where the splashing and thrashing was loudest. Mist still shrouded any sight of its cause. Josh stayed close to Uncle Charlie. His heart was thudding in his chest and his throat was dry from gulping in lungfuls of the cold morning air. Still they crouched low and edged forwards, until all that separated them from the source of the disturbance in the reeds was a tall knot of grasses. These Uncle Charlie parted with care, using the end of his stick. Josh was impressed: what if aliens *had* landed? Was his uncle fearless? Leaning forward, Uncle Charlie poked his head through the last few stalks – totally unprepared for the shock he was to receive.

Chapter 2

Since the young goose had landed, despite feeling dazed from the crash, it had rapidly become aware of several sensations: it was not exactly on water; one wing was twisted and pulsing with pain; and movement in any direction was impossible. Added to these problems, it felt the threat of something hiding close by. Its only means of defence lay in the strength of its long neck and bill. It used them to great effect when, suddenly, Uncle Charlie thrust his head through the tall grass. Instantly, the pointed beak zoomed like a bullet towards the poor man, before opening wide into a void that Uncle Charlie felt would swallow him whole. The creature hissed, spat and honked directly into his face, scaring him so much that he reeled backwards and landed on top of Josh. Together they toppled sideways into the shallow water, where they rolled about, disturbing the foul-smelling mud at the bottom. All the while, the goose continued to hiss and make a raucous sound like a rusty gate closing.

Dazed, Josh dragged himself to the bank before reaching out to help guide his uncle back to the edge.

"Did you *see* it?" Josh coughed out the words, spitting mud and weeds from his mouth. "What on *earth* is it?"

"*See* it!" exclaimed his uncle. "I almost *felt* it! *That* is one very angry goose."

"A *goose*!" exclaimed Josh. "Are you sure? It sounds like something much bigger, and far more ferocious."

"No doubt about it," his uncle puffed, still trying to catch his breath after the encounter. "It's definitely a goose. It seems vicious and angry, but I'm sure that's because it's extremely frightened, and only trying to defend itself. Poor thing! It's got one wing

tangled in fishing-line that someone has left caught in the reeds."

Josh winced. "That's *bad angling*, Uncle!" He knew how angered his uncle was by irresponsible anglers. Both Josh and Uncle Charlie had seen wildlife suffer before, because thoughtless anglers had left line in the water, or caught among reeds. Josh knew that sometimes it just wasn't possible to retrieve fishing-line from awkward places; his uncle had warned him that scrambling around near the water could be dangerous. But sadly there were people who fished without showing the slightest consideration for the ducks and birds living around the water. Their discarded fishing-line, weights, hooks, or even litter could cause needless suffering to the creatures.

"The wing is caught at a horrible angle," continued Uncle Charlie.

"What are we going to do about it, Uncle? We *can't* leave the poor thing here to suffer."

Uncle Charlie looked perplexed. He rubbed his hands to remove some of the foul-smelling mud that was beginning to dry.

"If we call out a vet, or find the water bailiff, the decision may be to put it down. The only other course of action is for *us* to retrieve it from the reeds and get it to a vet or sanctuary somewhere. But I certainly don't fancy losing my nose in a rescue attempt – it would only take one peck from that creature!"

Josh looked thoughtful, then said, "What if we crept up on the goose, managed to get the landing-net over its head and cut the line? Then, we could wrap a groundsheet around it and carry it to your van. There's an animal shelter a few miles away. *Please*, let's give it a try. They've saved all sorts of animals my friends have taken to them: stray cats, birds – even field mice!"

"I'm sure they have plenty of experience, Josh – but a wild goose? That might be a bit unusual for them," Uncle Charlie commented. He saw the worried expression on his nephew's face and, realizing they had to do something about the plight of the poor goose, accepted Josh's idea. It was better than anything else he could think of at that moment. He said, "We'll try to get it to the animal shelter, and see what they have to say. One thing's for certain, we *must* cut the fishing-line soon before the goose becomes more entangled." Uncle Charlie stood up, sneezed and shivered. "I thought we'd be catching the carp today," he sighed. "Instead, it looks as though we've probably caught colds!"

Chapter 3

From where the goose lay stranded in the reeds, it could hear the sounds of Josh and Uncle Charlie shifting about and talking. Uncle Charlie was right: the goose was afraid. But it wasn't the sound of ducks, their quacks sounding like hysterical laughter, or the sensation of fish moving below in the foul-smelling, grey water that bothered it. For the poor creature, it was the unpredictable movements of the intruders that made its pulse race. Were they heading in its direction again? Never before in its short life had it been so near to humans. Lowering its graceful head and pushing its sharp bill into the reeds, it tried, as much as possible, to keep out of sight. With its head bowed, the goose noticed a scattering of its own soft, grey plumage, which had been torn out by the fishing-line. It pecked at the line in an attempt to free its painful wing, but without success. Reluctantly, the goose felt the need to rest. It stayed quiet, although still alert.

This was not how the beautiful creature had expected its first real venture from home to have ended. By now, the other geese would be congregating on the huge lake. When the sun penetrated the morning mist to warm the earth, they would sit and groom themselves. Bending their long, elegant necks, they would dip their shining bills into the water, allowing its coolness to trickle down their throats and refresh them. The geese at home on the lake would be watching the sky, anticipating the return of the goose who had flown off alone. But they would wait in vain to see it land on the vast lake where it belonged.

Chapter 4

It occurred to Uncle Charlie that Josh's idea of using the landing-net and groundsheet in the rescue attempt was a pretty good way of tackling the problem.

"You're right, Josh," said Uncle Charlie. "As long as the goose's beak is covered by the net, it shouldn't be able to put up too much of a struggle while I cut the line free."

Josh waited while his uncle crept back to fetch the landing-net and groundsheet. Both Josh and Uncle Charlie felt very chilled from their dip in the muddy pond, but once they had agreed upon their roles in the rescue, they set to work without giving their discomfort a second thought. Wearing cold, soggy clothes, which gave off a horrible smell from the thick grey mud, didn't seem to bother them in the least.

The goose still lay with its head low, fearful of the slightest sound. It had made another feeble attempt to peck at the taut fishing line, but the line was too strong even for the goose's sharp beak.

Nearby, the other creatures seemed to be listening. There was a hush from their activities around the water, as though they sensed something unusual was happening in their territory.

Uncle Charlie and Josh slithered forwards on their stomachs through the reeds, like crocodiles slowly easing their way towards their prey. When they were only several arms' lengths away from the goose, the poor creature sensed their nearness and, terrified, swung its neck from side to side in a desperate attempt to warn them off. Its heart was beating wildly within the soft down of its chest. Uncle Charlie and Josh needed to act swiftly and efficiently, if they were to avoid alarming the goose any further.

At a given sign, Josh passed the landing-net on its long pole to his uncle. This time, the goose was taken by surprise before it had a chance to use its beak. Springing from the reeds, Uncle Charlie managed to jiggle the net over the goose's head and neck, ensuring the powerful beak was covered. Handing the pole to Josh, who took a firm hold of it to keep it steady, his uncle then restrained the goose while he cut the fishing-line with his penknife.

With the landing-net still in place over the goose's head and neck, they were able to cover the creature with the groundsheet and, between them, carry the goose to the bank. Pausing only to catch their breath, they then rushed the precious bundle to Uncle Charlie's old van, parked nearby, and laid it with care in the back of the vehicle. When the doors were closed, Josh peered through the windows. He became afraid when he saw how still the bundle lay. Even when Uncle Charlie opened one of the doors and managed to remove the landing-net from beneath the groundsheet, there was still no sign of movement.

"Oh *no*, Uncle! We've scared it to death," Josh exclaimed, beginning to wish he had stayed in bed that morning, and never set eyes on the pond.

"The poor thing's probably suffering from shock," Uncle Charlie replied. "Imagine how you would feel if someone threw a landing-net over your head and bundled you into the back of a van."

"I couldn't feel any worse than I do at the moment," Josh sighed, worried that his idea of rescuing the goose had worsened the situation.

"Just give it a few minutes to recover," said Uncle Charlie reassuringly, as he squeezed water from his trouser bottoms.

A few minutes passed, followed by ten more, without as much as a twitch from beneath the groundsheet. It was time to investigate. Cautiously opening the back of the van, Uncle Charlie lifted a corner of the sheet. Josh peered in; he was eager to see. This time, there was no hissing, honking monster jabbing its beak at him. Neither was there any sign of strength in the creature's

21

neck, which before had writhed like a giant snake, lunging unpredictably at its enemy. Instead, Uncle Charlie and Josh found themselves staring down at a rather pathetic, and tatty, young goose. Frightened and in pain, it was unable to lift its head to focus on its captors.

It seemed to be barely alive. Only one part of its body registered any movement at all: the small, dark eye it kept fixed upon Uncle Charlie and Josh. Its limp, dark-grey feathered neck lay stretched out along the van floor, and one wing stuck upward like a sail, at an awkward angle. Feathers had been torn from the wing's delicate structure by the fishing-line. The goose's black, rubbery feet looked sadly comical, as they protruded from beneath its body, appearing stiff and lifeless. Josh moved closer to gain a better view of the injured wing. Full of compassion, he acted upon impulse and extended a hand towards the goose's head. Uncle Charlie tried to restrain him, but was amazed when the creature appeared to show no fear of Josh – almost welcoming his touch. Gently, the boy stroked the goose's soft head and very soon the pathetic creature closed its eyes in sleep.

"I've seen lots of geese like this one in the park, Uncle," whispered Josh. "Can I sit with it in the back of the van, while you drive to the animal shelter?" Josh was already beginning to shift himself in next to the goose, but Uncle Charlie refused his request, insisting he sat next to him in the front.

Uncle Charlie had been surprised by the creature's reaction to his nephew: no fear, just a sense of trust in the boy. He knew his nephew loved animals – perhaps the goose felt that too. Sadly, when Uncle Charlie looked a little closer at the poor creature, he realized just how feeble it appeared to be. He hoped it was only sleeping, not slipping from life. Rushing back to the pond, he soon retrieved his fishing tackle from the bank and returned to stow it in the front of the van, so as not to disturb the goose.

Throughout the journey to the animal shelter, the goose remained still and silent; its eyes were closed. But when Uncle Charlie turned a corner a little too sharply, and the goose slid across the van floor, it suddenly opened its eyes wide in terror. Josh reached out a hand to stroke its head in an attempt to comfort it. He managed to calm the poor thing for the rest of the journey, but sat thinking how confused the wild creature must be. One moment it had felt free, soaring through the sharp morning air; the next, it lay bundled up in the back of an old van, passing through places so very different from those it knew.

The animal shelter opened soon after they arrived. Uncle Charlie spent only a few minutes in its reception, before appearing at the door with a tall, young man: the vet on duty. Uncle Charlie unlocked the back doors of the van, so that the young man was able to peer in and see the goose. Josh was stroking its head.

"I think we'll need to carry it in," said the vet. "With the wing stuck at that angle, it'll be difficult fitting it into any of our cages."

Taking great care not to alarm the goose any more than was necessary, Josh covered it with the groundsheet. Then, between them, all three manoeuvred it into an examination room. There they laid it on a high rubber-topped table. The injured wing still remained open like a feathered fan. When the young vet attempted to examine the injury, the goose summoned enough strength to hiss at him, before burying its head deep in Josh's jumper. Josh was pleased the goose had turned to him, once again, for comfort.

"It seems to feel safer with you around," stated the young vet. "Do you think you could stay close to it while I make my examination? It would certainly make the job easier."

Only too pleased to be of assistance, Josh did as he'd been requested. Gently prising apart the delicate plumage, the vet examined the injury. Then, taking some tiny scissors, he carefully snipped away at the entangled line. The goose hissed at him, yet again, when a particularly long piece of line was eased out. Letting a long, slow breath escape between pursed lips, the vet sighed.

"Such a shame. We're looking at a young, male Canada goose – healthy, too, apart from the injury and shock he's suffering. I very much doubt if he'll be taking to the sky again,

even if we are able to patch him up."

"Never fly - *ever* again!" exclaimed Josh, horrified that the accident caused by the discarded fishing-line had put an end to such a necessary part of the goose's life.

"I doubt it," the young vet replied. "But wildfowl *can* survive accidents like this and, providing they're able to find food and protect themselves, exist quite comfortably."

Josh continued to look worried, already feeling a closeness developing for the goose. He thought it a tragedy that a creature created for the sky should be confined to the ground. Josh began to wonder whether he was so fond of angling, after all. Was anything worth this sort of outcome?

The vet stopped cutting the fishing-line. "It's difficult to predict the outcome of any injured wild creature," he commented, aware of the expression of concern on Josh's face. "They can rally round surprisingly quickly if they're normally fit and healthy, and the injury isn't too severe." The vet stood back a few paces and looked at the goose's wing before announcing: "It's going to take quite a while, but I think I can remove the bits of line that have torn deeply into the wing, and tugged it at an angle. That should ease it down, making it more comfortable. We'll see how he fares, and if all goes well, he could live out his days in a wildfowl sanctuary."

The vet explained that he would continue to work on the wing, but first he went off to contact two sanctuaries; one of them would surely take the goose.

The goose was afraid. He had plunged from the sky into a strange world full of unfamiliar sights and sounds. But in his pain and confusion his instincts had turned him to Josh, where he found reassurance and protection. The boy was full of compassion for the helpless creature.

There was a perplexed expression on the young vet's face when he returned. "Slight problem," he said. "One place definitely can't take him. The other, in Dorset, has more casualties than they can handle at present; but they're prepared to have him if he recovers enough to fend for himself. Unfortunately we're not equipped to keep him here until then. If all goes well, he'll need room to exercise that wing, until he's strong enough to be transferred to the sanctuary. It's far too cramped for space here."

"That's no problem!" Josh piped up. "The goose can stay with my mum and me." He beamed with pleasure at the simplicity of his solution. But Josh's smile soon disappeared when Uncle Charlie explained that a flat without a garden wasn't exactly an ideal environment to shelter a goose. The young vet spoke up:

"Look, you've done your bit in helping the poor thing; leave it to me to find some way around the problem."

It seemed strange to Josh that he was to be parted from the goose so soon. He felt as though he was, somehow, meant to see more of him, but there was nothing more he could do to make that happen. He just wanted the goose to survive and wished he could be around to help. Worried and disheartened, Josh bent to whisper goodbye to the goose, although he was reluctant to leave. Eventually, the boy slouched away behind his uncle.

It wasn't until they were inside the van that Uncle Charlie turned to face Josh and saw sadness and disappointment in his nephew's features. Uncle Charlie sat deep in thought for a minute, cupping his chin in a grubby hand. Then, suspecting the peace of his retirement was about to end, he gave in to his feelings for Josh.

"*All right!*" he exclaimed. "*I'll* take the goose. But I'm warning you, Josh, if I'm unable to cope – he'll have to go."

The boy's eyes opened wide as he shouted in his uncle's face, "Uncle Charlie, you're *brilliant!*"

The young vet was pleased and relieved to know that Uncle Charlie had decided to care for the goose for a short time. If he was successful in removing the rest of the fishing-line, Uncle Charlie and Josh could collect the goose the next afternoon. Somewhere warm and quiet would be needed for the creature to rest and recover from the shock of the accident. Uncle Charlie told the young man that he had a garage at home, which he had converted into a sort of den. It was warm and spacious. With a few adjustments, the goose would have room to move about until ready to go outside. Uncle Charlie commented that his allotment, at the end of his garden, would come in very useful for that purpose. It even had a cosy shed where the goose could bed down at night.

Josh and his uncle left the shelter with their hands full of pamphlets containing information on all sorts of birds and wildfowl. Josh read some of the leaflets while his uncle drove him home to the little ground-floor flat Josh shared with his mother. Reading the information helped to keep him from thinking about the hours that lay ahead for the goose. He had been amazed by the goose's reaction to him and felt honoured: a wild creature had turned to him alone for comfort. The dark, glass-like eye had stared up at him, and instinct had told the goose that the boy meant him no harm.

*   *   *

With quick, skilful hands the young vet removed all traces of the deeply-embedded fishing-line, but as he had suspected, it was doubtful the goose would ever fly properly again. Exhausted and confused from the ordeal of the day, the goose lay cocooned in one of three small, warm enclosures at the back of the shelter.

The unfamiliar surroundings made the goose feel uneasy. He pecked at the wire enclosure, until the effort made pain pulse around the site of his injury. Both his legs were stiff, too, and ached from remaining in the same position for so long while he had slept. With sky and open water gone from his view, he felt lonely and fearful of the strange world he now inhabited. He was ill-prepared for a sterile environment, empty of bird calls and damp, earthy ground beneath his feet. Only the boy who had stroked his head had made him feel safe and secure. Tired from the effort of trying to make sense of the strange world, he dozed, then slept once more.

Chapter 5

"**H**e's been asleep for hours," announced the young vet. It was late in the afternoon of the next day. Josh had been eager to return to the shelter and hear about the goose. A telephone call to the vet that morning had, at least, put his mind at rest that the creature still lived. The hours had passed too slowly for Josh, until it was time to go to the shelter.

"Seems to have come through pretty well. That wing will cause him some discomfort for a while, but I'm hopeful that he'll be up and about very soon. Try to persuade him to eat over the next few days; he'll need to build up his strength."

Josh knelt at the side of the wire enclosure.

He managed to squeeze a finger through a gap so that he could stroke the goose's tail feathers. He could see the wing the vet had worked on. So many of the feathers had been removed that he was reminded of pictures in a book depicting bird skeletons. The wing looked very sore, but Josh was relieved to see that it no longer stuck upwards. As though suddenly aware of the activity around him, the goose opened his eyes. The first thing that came into focus was Josh.

The young vet and Uncle Charlie managed to transfer the drowsy goose into a carrier which could be used for transporting him, now that the injured wing no longer stuck out at an angle. Josh carried a supply of food supplements for the goose to the van. These were vital for helping him to regain his strength and stamina. He needed the sort of nutrients he would find in the wild. The vet decided he would discuss the goose's move to the sanctuary when Uncle Charlie reported back to him that the creature was showing positive signs of improvement. If, on the other hand, the goose became weaker, Uncle

Charlie was to contact the animal shelter immediately.

With the precious cargo safely installed in the back of the van, Uncle Charlie took the journey home at a slow pace, taking care not to hit too many bumps in the road. Josh watched the goose throughout the entire journey to reassure him. The goose stared right back at him through dark, watery eyes, rarely letting his attention drop.

As they made their way through the streets, Josh decided to keep his uncle informed on the subject of "The Canada Goose". He had read all the vet's leaflets and had spent the last evening in his local library, scouring the wildlife section, for more information.

"Did you know, Uncle Charlie," he announced from the back of the van, "that the Canada goose was introduced into this country from North America, and has bred here for three hundred years? It can be extremely tame, but is also known to display aggression, especially when defending its nest. The female lays five to six eggs. Nine weeks after they hatch," Josh continued, sounding as though he'd memorized an entire chapter of a book, "they become soft, downy young fledglings."

Uncle Charlie smiled to himself, amazed by Josh's sudden knowledge. There was no doubt that the goose had captured his nephew's interest. He only hoped Josh wouldn't get too attached to him. As a wild creature, it was only right that he be returned to his natural habitat, providing he was capable of fending for himself.

"*And* – I bet you didn't know," Josh went on, "that the Canada goose is known to live in flocks of up to a thousand birds. They usually build their nests around the edge of lakes, ponds, or other stretches of water. Often they take to the air, with a loud trumpeting cry, like this: *AARGH-HONK!*"

The sudden loud squawk, released from Josh's throat, took Uncle Charlie by surprise and almost caused him to swerve. Even the goose turned his head in the direction of Josh's call, and looked bewildered.

"*See!* He knows. He thinks I'm one of the flock," exclaimed Josh, delighted that his impression should bring about such a reaction.

Uncle Charlie had devoted several hours to preparing his snug den in the garage for the feathered visitor. He had pushed most of the usual clutter of old furniture, magazines and fishing equipment to one side and spread sheets of polythene over the floor. This would make the job of cleaning up after the goose each day much easier.

In a freshly-swept corner, under his work bench, Uncle Charlie had made a makeshift nest for the goose. Cleverly constructed from an old, broken picnic-hamper and lined with strips of blanket and straw, it looked very cosy. He had placed two large bowls nearby: one for fresh drinking water and the other for the goose's food.

An inquisitive neighbour, with a frosty expression, peered through her immaculate, white lace curtains as Uncle Charlie and Josh manoeuvred the big cage through the front door. Carefully they carried it out to the kitchen, where they rested their aching backs for a few minutes.

"Don't you think he should spend the first

day and night indoors with us, Uncle? Could get pretty lonely out there," Josh commented, hoping his uncle would allow the goose to stay in the house.

Uncle Charlie smiled, but shook his head in disapproval of the suggestion, and returned to the job of moving the goose into the den. Josh helped his uncle to ease the goose gently out of the cage and on to the nest. The goose seemed docile and, as long as Josh was close by, permitted himself to be shifted around until the best, and most comfortable, position for him was found. Josh scooped some of the special food into the bowl and placed it in front of the creature. The goose looked at it for a few moments, but didn't attempt to eat.

Given the opportunity, Josh would have stayed close by the goose throughout the rest of the day, and all of the night, too. As it was the school holidays, Josh was allowed, like most other holidays, to stay with his uncle. With the arrival of the goose, Josh anticipated that it could be an extra-special holiday. Before tea, he set to work on making a chart so that he could record any changes in the goose's health. He ruled spaces where he could enter when the goose ate, drank, or was active in some way.

Before settling down for the night, Josh headed for Uncle Charlie's den to look in on the goose. He was disappointed to see that not one mouthful of the food had been touched, and the level of water in the other bowl remained the same. The goose was drowsy, although his eyes still followed every move the boy made. Josh picked up the chart, with its little red pencil attached to it by a short length of string, and put a "No" in the columns indicating food and water. Under the heading of "activities" he recorded: "Goose quiet and sleepy."

Taking care not to alarm the goose, Josh retreated from the garage. In the half-light, two dark, mysterious eyes took a long look around at their surroundings. Seeing no immediate danger, the goose closed his heavy lids and slipped into a deep sleep.

Chapter 6

Josh sat up in bed. He had been dreaming and his forehead was damp with sweat. In his dream he'd been cutting his way through fine webs of fishing-line, trying to reach the injured goose. Whenever he'd thought he was making progress, more line had appeared to bar his way.

Josh pushed aside the thick layers of blankets, stood up giddily, and staggered to the window. He rubbed his eyes. It was very early in the morning. Outside, a thin layer of frost coated the garden. It covered everything in a shimmering, pale blue light, which fuzzed the edges of objects like Uncle Charlie's trousers hanging on the clothes-line. Josh thought they looked spooky when they moved with the slightest breeze. He walked back to the little camp bed that his uncle put up for him whenever he stayed. Sitting on the edge of it, Josh considered whether the dream had been a warning. Perhaps the goose was in some kind of danger – at that very moment drifting away from its short life? Josh thrust his feet into his boots and pulled on a jumper.

In the kitchen he reached for the keys and unlocked the back door, taking care not to wake his uncle. Three almost silent footsteps took him to the den. Using another key, he let himself in. Fearing the worst, his dream still tormenting him, Josh tiptoed over to the goose's makeshift nest, and crouched down. Although the light was dim, he was still able to make out the gentle rise and fall of the goose's soft chest. He slept soundly; all was well. Thank goodness – the dream had been proved wrong.

Josh looked at the goose, taking in all the details of its plumage. Even with the damaged wing, he thought the creature looked magnificent. He was definitely a young one, fitting well the description and drawing in one of the library books. Just like the drawing, the smoky-grey feathers turned darker grey around the face; everything was exactly right. Josh yawned, feeling sleepy again. He pulled the jumper down over his knees and curled up close to the goose. Soon, he too was asleep. This time, it was a dreamless, undisturbed sleep.

An hour or so later, the goose opened his eyes. He was startled to discover someone lying next to him, until he realized it was Josh. He looked around and, when his glance fell on the two bowls, stretched his neck towards the one full of water. The black bill opened and he sipped a few refreshing drops. Josh stirred in his sleep, and the goose leaned his neck against him, sensing safety in the boy's presence.

When Uncle Charlie entered his den, several hours later, he wasn't in the least surprised to find Josh with the goose. They looked so cosy that he left them and tiptoed back to the house.

* * *

Throughout the day Josh made frequent visits to the den, refilling the goose's water bowl and replacing the special food in the food dish. Josh was delighted to see that towards the end of the day the goose had taken water and food, between long periods of dozing. Still tired and confused after his ordeal, he had begun to seem more settled and comfortable. He had even made a few attempts to groom the feathers on his good wing. Josh was pleased to be able to record these facts on the goose's chart – especially that he had seen the goose nuzzling the feathers into shape.

The boy was so happy to see improvement in the goose. He began to wonder how long it would be before the creature was up on his feet.

Chapter 7

"Did you hear that, Josh?" Uncle Charlie called to his nephew, who was dumping an armful of brambles on the compost heap at the end of the garden. It was late in the afternoon of the next day. Uncle Charlie thought he had heard the sound of breaking glass. Josh shook his head; he hadn't heard it. Both of them returned to their chores.

"I heard *that*!" Josh suddenly exclaimed, as he and Uncle Charlie headed, at speed, towards the den. Several loud crashes had come from that direction. Josh was first on the scene. As he opened the door, his eyes darted to the goose's nest. But the goose wasn't there! Josh surveyed the rest of the den, terrified of what might have befallen the unfortunate creature, who had suffered more than enough already. Uncle Charlie arrived moments later, took one look, and slumped against the door frame as he shut his eyes to block out the scene.

The den was in chaos: broken bottles; upturned tins of paint; jars, smashed and oozing their oily contents; books; fishing tackle; and a variety of objects in need of repair – all littered the floor in colourful disarray. Uncle Charlie took an audible deep breath, then sighed it out through clenched teeth. Josh panicked; he still couldn't see the goose anywhere. "Uncle, he's *gone*! The goose has escaped!"

Uncle Charlie half-opened his eyes and pointed, with an index finger, to a corner of the den. "No, Josh. He's not *gone* – just *camouflaged*!"

Josh focused on the corner. Squatting on top of a pile of old fishing magazines, with his plumage featuring most of the colours of the rainbow, was the goose.

After long periods of sleep and some healthy

nourishment, the goose had felt a sudden surge of energy and a taste for living return to his body. He was still weak, but his instinct to survive had risen to the surface. For the first time in days, and in spite of shaky limbs and a useless wing, he had used all his willpower to raise himself until he stood on both legs.

His neck no longer drooped – it was held up straight – and although his surroundings still seemed strange and disorientating, he had begun to regain a sense of just what sort of creature he was. Inquisitive about all that lay around him, and feeling a need to investigate, he had inspected the den – with disastrous results.

Trailing the injured wing at his side, he had at first found walking a little difficult. His legs were wobbly from lack of use, but he'd staggered about where Uncle Charlie kept remnants of paint and liquids left over from decorating jobs around the house. A few had toppled over, when he'd accidentally bumped into them; some of their contents had spilled on the floor. At first, the mess hadn't bothered the goose; he was too busy enjoying the

freedom of being able to explore. As confidence had returned to his legs, he'd adjusted his balance and taken himself off to make a thorough inspection of all the areas in his new home.

Having waddled over to satisfy his curiosity about the liquid inside a particularly large jar, the goose had plunged his inquisitive beak into its depths. Instantly offended by the strong odour, he had withdrawn his head and sent the jar and its contents crashing across the floor. He'd then moved on to several other containers, examining them in the same manner.

It hadn't been long before the goose had found himself wading, ankle deep, in a mixture of paint, turpentine and other cleaning fluids. Pretty patterns of his footprints had soon covered the floor. Despite the unpleasant odours, he had enjoyed his exploration, until the thickness of paint in which he'd trodden started to slow his progress. He had begun to panic when it became difficult for him to lift his feet. Using his good wing as best he could, he'd managed to produce a flapping and hopping movement, which eventually took him up on to a box which supported a mirror intended for renovation. Suddenly confronted by the image of a terrifying, brightly-coloured waterfowl, he had hissed and pecked at his reflection. Defeated by the attack, the mirror had tumbled with a series of resounding crashes to the floor, where it had splintered into numerous fragments. The goose had stood triumphant, but exhausted and suddenly weak. As his surroundings had begun to spin before his eyes, he'd toppled giddily from the box. Floundering in the thick carpet of paint, he had finally retreated to hide in a corner, at the sound of approaching footsteps.

Several hours of cleaning and tidying the mess still hadn't dampened Josh's enthusiasm for the creature.

"At least we can see he's made a big improvement, Uncle," said Josh, smiling, as he emptied the last bucketful of rainbow-coloured water down the drain. Uncle Charlie was much less enthusiastic.

"The sooner I make the shed ready for the goose, the better for *all* of us," he grumbled. He gazed down at a treasured old clock he had looked forward to repairing. It would take him hours to remove the pink, yellow and green paint from its face. He decided to discard it, wondering, if he was honest with himself, whether he would ever have got round to fixing it. He considered, for a moment, that in a strange way the goose had done him a favour: so much of the old clutter had been ruined by paint, it would have to be discarded. Uncle Charlie knew how hard he found it to throw anything away; he was, by nature, a hoarder. For a long while he had intended to clear out any unnecessary items in the den. The trouble was, he couldn't decide just what should go, and what could be allowed to stay. Now the goose had solved the problem for him; the den was free of a lot of clutter.

Cleaning the goose proved to be considerably more difficult than clearing up the chaos it had caused. The gloss paint was incredibly hard to remove because Uncle Charlie was reluctant to use anything containing chemicals on the goose's plumage. Gently dabbing at the feathers with warm water, Josh patiently coaxed some of it off; the rest, he hoped, would eventually wear off.

Chapter 8

Josh continued to log the goose's feeding and activities. By the end of the week, the creature looked less colourful. Mostly, this had been achieved by preening. The goose had begun to show pleasure whenever Josh or his uncle entered the den – especially when it was Josh. He did this by producing a strange clacking noise with his beak. Sometimes, he would make a show of pecking odd bits of straw from his bedding.

Uncle Charlie decided it was time to move the goose into the shed on the allotment. He felt the move would have a beneficial effect upon the creature, putting him in touch with life out in the open once again. The smell of vegetation; the trickle of water from a tiny stream running along one side of the allotments; and the rustle of wind among the trees – all these could hasten the goose's healing process. They were sounds and sensations Uncle Charlie imagined to be closer to those of the goose's natural environment.

The allotment, like all the others, had a thin chicken-wire fence marking its boundaries. Most of the allotment owners grew a few flowers and shrubs, but vegetables were the main feature of the small, flourishing plots. If Uncle Charlie could keep the slugs at bay, he was usually able to provide himself with lettuces in the summer months. One year, he had even produced a healthy crop of pungent tomatoes; they had tasted so good to him and he was very proud of his achievement. But Uncle Charlie derived his greatest pleasure from his little plot of land simply by sinking his spade into the dark, grey earth and digging. As long as the ground wasn't too hard with frost, Uncle Charlie loved nothing better (except perhaps fishing) than to dig.

In contrast to Uncle Charlie's relaxed

attitude to his patch of land, his neighbours on either side produced vegetables as though they were laying up supplies for a lengthy siege. Huge marrows, velvety-leaved cabbages in emerald and mauve hues, onions as perfect and unblemished as a brand new cricket ball – all kinds of vegetables flourished on their land. And the reason for growing such perfection: the annual Local Home Produce Competition. Held at the town hall, it was always presided over by the mayor who awarded gleaming cups, trophies and rosettes to the champion growers.

The neighbour who lived to Uncle Charlie's left was called William. Residing on Uncle Charlie's right was Ben. Like Uncle Charlie they reached their allotments through gates at the bottom of their gardens. William and Ben existed in fierce competition with one another as to who could collect the most awards at the annual show. Both had gained more or less the same amount of trophies over the years. But as time went by, and they grew older, the need to prove beyond doubt that one was a superior gardener to the other increased to a point of undeclared war. Uncle Charlie's allotment looked quite barren, standing between the incredible displays of Ben's turnips and William's prized marrows that lay like great, green insect larvae, ripe to pop at any moment. Both neighbours had made Uncle Charlie handsome offers for his plot of land, so that they could extend their own areas for growing more of their winning varieties, but he had happily declined. His little patch of land was far too precious to him for his own purpose. When Uncle Charlie needed to think over a problem, or just relax, he found digging to be a great comfort.

It was decided that late evening was probably the best time to install the goose in the shed. Supervised, he could wander around the allotment for a while, before being closed in for the night. William and Ben had put in appearances in their gardens while Uncle Charlie and Josh were feeding the goose on the allotment. Both men had expressed fear that the goose could harm their precious vegetables. Uncle Charlie had attempted to dispel their worries, explaining how well he had checked to ensure his fences were secure. He told them it was extremely unlikely that a goose with a badly-injured wing would be causing any trouble (conveniently forgetting the incident in his den). Still, his neighbours mumbled and grumbled as they went about overseeing the tending of their immaculate crops.

The fresh air seemed to stimulate the goose to eat larger amounts of his special food, and the soft earth beneath his feet pleased him, encouraging him to take exercise. The injured wing was still thin and lace-like where feathers were missing and although it now trailed limply at his side, there was no mistaking a new liveliness in his step. Like a guard on duty he patrolled up and down Uncle Charlie's allotment.

Earlier that evening William and Ben had spent two hours in their allotments. Minute weeds had been carefully extracted from per-fectly nourished soil, before being plunged into bin liners for disposal. Each rival had gone about the task of tending his prize vegetables, while trying not to appear in the least interested in the other's activities. This was far from the truth.

William and Ben always went to great lengths to avoid speaking to one another. But that day they had found themselves in a situation where it had been difficult for either of them to remain silent. To William's horror, he had found a weed protruding through Uncle Charlie's fence, daring to trespass on his sacred plot. Indignantly, he had stooped to remove the offending growth, and thrown it back in the direction of Uncle Charlie's land. By chance, a gust of wind had caught the weed and carried it further. It had landed, as light as a feather, on one of Ben's prized crops. Seizing the weed and dangling it in the air between gardening-gloved thumb and forefinger, Ben had raised himself to confront his neighbour over the fence. Imagining his rival had hurled the weed in a moment of spite, he said,

"It appears you have dropped one of your *leeks*!"

William had been puzzled for a moment, before realizing what must have happened. He'd been about to offer an explanation, but instead, angered by Ben's sarcastic remark, replied curtly,

"Forgive me. I mistook it for one of *yours* – I was merely returning it." Not another word was spoken by either man – war, on a grand scale, had begun.

If the truth was known, William despised Ben, who was always so ready to suspect him if anything went awry on his plot. But William felt sure that before the year was out, revenge and victory over Ben would be sweet. He was positive his own entries for the annual show that year would win the most cups, making him the undisputed champion.

Breathing fresh air, rather than the strange smells in the den, made the goose quite excited. It was obvious he enjoyed the freedom of waddling around the allotment: inspecting an interesting corner here, and dipping his beak into something green and slimy there. When he saw Josh pulling a few weeds from the ground, he attempted to imitate the boy's actions. Josh laughed to see him tugging at the weeds, his beak earthy from the struggle. He was even happier to see how strong the goose was becoming.

The shed was ready: the makeshift nest had been installed, and food and water had been put down. Uncle Charlie made another thorough inspection of the fence on all sides of his land. Meanwhile, Josh led the goose into the shed and sat with him, stroking his soft head and speaking quietly, reassuring him of his new surroundings. He didn't want the goose to feel afraid of yet another move. The goose soon slept soundly, comfortably tired from his labour on the allotment. Uncle Charlie ensured the latch on the old door was securely closed.

"That should do the trick, Josh," he whispered. "I don't think he'll be able to get out – and if he did, there's no way he could fly over the fence."

Chapter 9

A cry of anguish had Josh and Uncle Charlie leaping from their beds early the next morning. Reaching for their dressing-gowns, they rushed to the back garden where the ghoulish shriek seemed to have originated. One thought was uppermost in Josh's mind: had the goose got out and attacked a neighbour? But when they reached the allotment, they were relieved to find the shed door was still shut. Peeping through the window, they both saw the goose curled up and quietly dozing. Everything appeared to be normal. Josh and Uncle Charlie were puzzled; they had both heard the same blood-curdling cry coming from the allotments.

Other neighbours had also been alerted by the sound; they were peering through their curtains to investigate, but there was nothing out of the ordinary to be seen.

Bare feet sank into damp earth as Uncle Charlie and Josh made their way back to the house, but they were soon halted in their tracks by a deep moaning sound. It came from ground level on Ben's allotment. Uncle Charlie and Josh crept noiselessly back to the allotments, found a small gap in a row of neatly-planted shrubs on Ben's side of the fence, and peered through. There, they saw the pathetic sight of their neighbour, Ben. Wearing little more than a pair of striped pyjamas, and slippers, he knelt among the wreckage of his prize turnip patch, cradling one of the huge specimens while repeatedly wailing to himself, "How could he? How *could* he?"

Ben's wife eventually appeared in her dressing-gown and led her husband back inside their house, while Uncle Charlie leaned over the fence to inspect the damaged patch. For no apparent reason, someone had destroyed nearly all of the perfectly-formed turnips. They had been tossed about the allotment; in some places, they were trampled beyond recognition. Uncle Charlie thought it a mystery, until later, when he called on Ben and heard him relate the incident of the previous evening concerning William and the weed. Uncle Charlie then paid William a visit. The man swore he had taken no part in the wrecking of Ben's turnips. But nothing could persuade Ben *not* to believe that only William, his envious neighbour, could be capable of such a devious act, especially since they had exchanged words.

Uncle Charlie didn't see much of Josh that day. He was too busy dashing between his neighbours, trying like an amateur detective to solve the crime of the uprooted turnips. Josh was able to devote all of his time to the goose during his uncle's absence. He was delighted to find the creature his constant companion. When Josh went into the kitchen to make a sandwich, the goose followed him as far as the back door, where he sat and waited patiently. Having constructed a monstrous snack, made from two wedges of bread and all sorts of ingredients found in his uncle's fridge, Josh cut a slice of bread for the goose. He sat on the kitchen step, throwing bits of the bread to the goose, who after a few attempts managed to catch the pieces in his beak before they fell to the ground.

How happy Josh felt to see the goose performing so well; the injured wing didn't seem to bother him. Josh munched his way through his sandwich, watching the goose and wondering what sort of future lay in store for him. He was aware that if the goose continued to show steady improvement he would go to the sanctuary all too soon. When Josh looked closely at the goose's face, he found it hard to accept that he was staring into the same features which had appeared so close to death not that long ago. It seemed a pity to Josh that the goose, who was apparently so content in his surroundings, would have to be moved to the sanctuary. But, more than anything, Josh wanted what was right for the goose: a wing, healed as well as possible, and the proper environment for him to develop into a fully-grown goose – even if these things meant he would have to be parted from the creature.

As Josh ate the last bit of his sandwich, the goose waddled over to him and settled at his feet. One rubbery foot rested on Josh's shoe. A dark eye as shiny as a marble looked up at the boy, who put out a hand to stroke the creature's soft head. Josh felt peaceful and wished the moment could last for ages. He thought how incredible it was that the beautiful goose had once hatched from an egg. He tried to imagine what strange sort of thing the goose must have appeared: all wobbly, with big eyes? He continued to stroke the goose's head, and puzzled as to whether the creature was missing his friends and family.

Uncle Charlie fell asleep in his armchair after tea that evening. Living in the middle of a war zone wasn't exactly how he had antici-pated the start of his early retirement. He made a mental note to spend more time fish-ing, once the goose had gone to the sanctuary.

With the goose settled for the night in the shed, Josh resisted the urge to sneak out and

look at him. Instead, he sat down to fill in his chart. Feeling pleased by his success with the goose, he entered a red tick in the sections for food and water. Under the activities column, he recorded: "Busy all day on allotment."

Chapter 10

Uncle Charlie sat in bed drinking a mug of tea. It was morning and he was considering whether he might take Josh for a few hours fishing on a canal, not too far away. It would do them good after the troubles of the previous day. He was mulling over the idea, wondering whether it would be safe to leave the goose, when he became aware of rain falling. Fishing would have to be abandoned; Josh's mum wasn't too keen for her son to sit on the side of a bank while rain beat down on him.

Uncle Charlie drew aside his curtains to see whether the sky foretold rain for the rest of the day. He was surprised to see a clear, blue sky without the slightest sign of rain or grey clouds. So why the sound of a downpour? He looked closely at the allotments – and soon found his answer. A heavy, steady jet of water appeared to spurt upwards from Ben's plot of land. It formed a perfect arch like a rainbow right over the top of Uncle Charlie's allotment before falling, fiercely but accurately, upon several rows of William's prized vegetables. Under the weight and ferocity of the well-aimed water, they were sinking slowly into the ground.

"*Josh!* Come *quickly!*" Uncle Charlie hollered to his nephew, who also thought he'd woken to a rainy day. Producing a wide yawn, Josh plodded upstairs to his uncle's bedroom. Through sleepy eyes he stared hard at the mysterious fountain of water. Uncle Charlie had already drawn conclusions.

"If those two are going to fight like schoolboys," he exclaimed, "then they're *not* going to do it over *my* patch of land – or our goose, for that matter!"

Josh and his uncle washed and dressed hurriedly to the sounds of angry cries which seemed to be coming from William's allotment. Uncle Charlie ran to the end of his garden and peered over the fence. One glance quickly revealed the extent of the damage caused by the fountain. Several rows of William's vegetables lay in a muddy pool; they were beyond saving. While William continued to rage, shouts of delight came from Ben's house. In his upstairs bedroom facing the allotments, Ben could be seen at his window. He was jumping up and down with excitement, obviously enjoying what he imagined to be the taste of revenge.

Two policemen stood on William's doorstep. They had been summoned by his wife to investigate accusations of Ben's unreasonable behaviour. The policemen took notes, then approached Ben to hear his side of the story. After conferring outside Ben's house, they concluded that the neighbours' feud was disturbing the peace. Both Ben and William could find themselves facing prosecution if it went any further. Terrified by the reprimand, and of the damage to their reputations as local gardening celebrities, the men stayed in their homes.

"Brave goose!" said Josh, as he refilled the water bowl and put down fresh food. "Weren't you afraid of those two, squabbling about a few old cabbages and turnips? Come out and stretch your legs. It's safe now."

The goose obediently followed Josh from the shed into the bright daylight. He seemed very alert, Josh noticed, especially when he hopped up on to an old wooden box and surveyed his little kingdom. Josh was amazed at the speed with which the goose was recovering. Secretly, he still dreaded the approach of the day when the creature would be moved to the wildfowl sanctuary.

Having been woken for two successive mornings to find his neighbours in dispute, Uncle Charlie woke even earlier the next day. He half-expected to open his curtains to reveal another scene of revenge. It was barely dawn. Only a few birds had begun to announce the beginning of a new day. Uncle Charlie padded, bare-footed, to his bedroom window. There was no noise, apart from the birds. No sound of wailing came from either William's or Ben's house. In fact, everything seemed very normal for that time of the morning. And yet – something bothered him. What a strange atmosphere. Nothing was out of place, but it seemed as though something was about to happen. Uncle Charlie continued to scrutinize the garden and the allotment until he found his vision drawn towards the goose's shed. The latch on the old door was rattling. Click! It lifted and the door swung open.

As though turned to stone, Uncle Charlie stood mesmerized, watching the goose step from the shed with an air of confidence and purpose in his stride. Having refreshed himself with a few sips of water from an old watering-can, the goose then proceeded to hop up on to an upturned bucket, close to Ben's fence, before using his good wing to flutter over into the neighbour's allotment. Once there, he proceeded to weed the lines of vegetables, making little distinction between what few weeds might exist, and the perfect

lines of wonderfully-formed specimens. His busy beak delved in among the crops, tugging and lifting them into the air, before shaking and dropping them to the ground.

Uncle Charlie's mouth fell open as he stood and watched the busy, muddy beak doing its worst. Revelling in his newly acquired skill as a gardener, the goose weeded in the same manner as he had seen Josh perform. All too quickly, the events of the past two days fell horribly into place in Uncle Charlie's mind.

Josh was very unhappy that morning. The first words he'd heard had been his uncle's description of the goose's activities on Ben's allotment. The culprit would have to be revealed. Josh's pulse was racing as he pleaded, in vain, with his uncle, trying to make him understand that the goose had learned to weed. Josh explained how he had laughed when he'd watched the goose copying him while he weeded on the allotment. Who could blame a goose if he couldn't tell vegetables from weeds? Uncle Charlie had been quick to point out that he doubted whether William or

Ben would see it quite that way. Terrified of the consequences, after hearing the bad news, Josh had obeyed his uncle and, at his request, gone to the allotment in the hope of luring the goose back into the shed.

When the goose spotted Josh leaning over the fence, quietly but insistently calling to him, he stopped his frantic weeding activities and gave his friendly beak-clacking welcome. Josh extended a hand and beckoned, whispering, "Why not come back to *your* allotment? I'll get your special food for you."

But the goose just clacked again; he was having far too much fun. Looking around, he spied one of the few turnips which remained on Ben's land after the first assault. Digging into the earth around its base, the goose then pulled at the root with his sharp beak. Josh broke out in a cold sweat. Uncle Charlie had sent him to bring the goose back, while he was working out the best way to break the dreadful news to his neighbours. Josh was petrified his uncle would come to the garden and witness the goose laying into the massive vegetable.

In a moment of panic, while the goose continued to show off his strength, Josh leapt over the fence and, remembering all he'd been taught at school about rugby tackles, hurled himself at the huge, earthy globe. Refusing to let go, Josh clung on to the turnip with all his strength, dragging it backwards to the fence. To his dismay, he realized the goose thought it all part of a game as, grasping the turnip even more firmly with his beak, he attempted to pull the thing away from Josh. Josh pulled back, and the goose, raising his good wing to help him balance, used all the power within his strong neck to tug against Josh.

The improvised tug o' war lasted for as long as it took Josh to move the goose and turnip, little by little, to the fence. Once there, still maintaining his grip, Josh managed to lure the goose back over the fence by way of the upturned bucket it had used to gain entry to Ben's allotment. The delighted creature, still far too involved in his attempt to win possession of the vegetable, obliged by entering the shed without any protest. There, he

proceeded to shred the remains of the turnip. Josh shut the door and wedged a box against it. He placed two old watering-cans on top of the box for extra security. There was no way he could allow the goose to escape again. Covered in William's rich earth, sweating and smelling strongly of turnip, the exhausted boy collapsed against the shed. Minutes later, when he left the allotment, he could still hear sounds of the goose engaged in his tussle with what little remained of the prize turnip.

Josh faced Uncle Charlie. Although he hadn't wanted his uncle to witness the battle for the turnip on Ben's allotment, he felt it necessary to be honest and tell Uncle Charlie just what had happened when he had attempted to retrieve the goose from William's land. Uncle Charlie was aghast.

"It gets worse, Josh. He'll have to go – and just as soon as I'm able to make the arrangements."

Uncle Charlie dreaded the prospect of revealing the probable culprit of the raid on Ben's prize turnips, which had in turn led to

Ben's watery revenge on William. There was also the matter of the goose's latest turnip raid, only that morning, which would require an explanation too. Uncle Charlie decided, as it was still very early, to wait until both his neighbours had risen before breaking the news to them. Any consideration for Josh and the goose had to be overlooked until he'd settled matters with the two men.

William and Ben sat at opposite ends of Uncle Charlie's front room. Staring angrily at one another, they listened intently to an account of the part the goose had played in the unfortunate activities of the past few days. To Uncle Charlie's amazement, by the time he had finished his confession, the two neighbours had undergone a transformation. From having been sworn enemies, they appeared, within a matter of minutes, to be the best of friends. They poured out profuse apologies for their hasty judgement of one another, while Uncle Charlie looked on, speechless. The two men smiled, joked and even offered to help one another put their allotments back in shape. Uncle Charlie couldn't believe his eyes, or his ears. Perhaps they weren't such bad neighbours after all. He had to admit, they'd taken the news very well. But his pleasure was short-lived. As he approached them to say how grateful he was that they'd accepted the unfortunate incident so well, both men suddenly turned their full vengeance upon him. William and Ben stated that they expected Uncle Charlie to pay, in full, for all the damage caused. Even if it took his very *last* penny – they knew their rights! As for the culprit, they were united in their decision. THE GOOSE HAD TO GO!

Chapter 11

Since the goose's performance in the morning, Josh had visited him only once, and that had been to take fresh food and water. When Josh had left, the goose had been prepared to follow him out of the shed. But to his surprise, the door had been firmly shut and the box replaced to keep it that way. Unhappy and feeling uncomfortable with the action he'd been forced to take, Josh had felt himself compelled to creep back and look in at the window. Peering in, he'd been saddened to see the goose standing by the door, waiting expectantly, his head on one side, for Josh's return. Josh had felt very sorry for him; the poor creature was confused. How was he expected to understand why his freedom on the allotment had been suddenly denied him?

Before the light faded that day, Josh wandered out to the shed once more. He was feeling unhappy with the news Uncle Charlie had just given him: the wildfowl sanctuary was able to take the goose the very next day. When his uncle had spoken to the vet at the animal shelter, informing him of the recent turn of events, the vet had been amazed at the speedy improvement the goose had shown. But, recognizing the urgency of the situation, he had made arrangements for the sanctuary to take the goose. As Josh opened the shed door he saw the goose resting quietly on his bedding. He tiptoed in and clicked the latch shut. Kneeling beside the beautiful creature, he thought the goose appeared a little wary of him; he was used to seeing Josh happy. The boy reached out and stroked the goose's head. He felt the need to talk to him. It didn't matter to Josh that the creature didn't understand the words – he knew the goose would feel his concern for him.

"Uncle Charlie said his neighbours are well within their rights to insist you go," he told the goose. "I know you're not aware of the problems we've caused by keeping you here, stuck between the two worst people to have around, if you happen to be a goose. But Uncle Charlie reckons that if you're strong enough to lift the latch, get over the fence and uproot Ben's turnips, then you're ready to take care of yourself at the sanctuary. We're to take you there tomorrow – but I *know* you don't want to leave us. And there's nothing on earth that would make me want you to go." Josh checked himself for a second. "Except, perhaps, knowing you'll have all the space you need to grow into an adult goose among other wild creatures. And Uncle Charlie won't need to wake up worrying, any more, about what the day has in store for him."

The goose dropped his head on one side, allowing one bright eye to focus on the boy. Josh felt uncomfortable. It was as though the goose had seen right through his words and sensed that he was to be moved away. For a moment, Josh considered smuggling the goose into his bedroom at the home he shared with his mum, but he realized it would be pointless; the goose would still end up being taken away.

Josh reflected on the days the goose had spent with him. He felt helpless and began to wish he hadn't been so keen to involve Uncle Charlie in caring for the goose. He was sorry that his uncle would have to pay out heavily to William and Ben. Josh was grieved by his uncle's situation. He sat stroking the smooth, grey-feathered head, each of them drawing comfort from the other's company. He picked up the chart he had kept faithfully, each day, since the goose had been at Uncle Charlie's house. Josh glanced at it, then dropped it to the floor. What did it matter any more? Someone else would be taking note of the goose's progress from now on.

The goose was dozing off to sleep. Josh whispered close to the soft head, before he left: "You're so much better now. Whatever happens, when you leave, just keep getting stronger – for me."

Chapter 12

It was misty when Uncle Charlie's van set off for the sanctuary early the next day – misty like the morning they had found the goose, Josh reflected. The old vehicle bounced and rumbled its way along the motorway, keeping to the inside lane, while much faster traffic swooshed past them. The journey seemed endless to Josh and he wasn't looking forward to being separated from the goose at the end of it.

Uncle Charlie fought to keep his car radio tuned, but like the car it was showing signs of age, and the crackling sound it emitted only served to annoy Josh. The goose slept most of the way. When he awoke he looked startled by his surroundings until his gaze fell upon Josh sitting in the front. The boy had little to say. He was saddened to think that every mile took him nearer to losing the creature who'd become so much part of his life for the past weeks.

"Hope their rotten leeks and lettuces get eaten by slugs," Josh eventually mumbled, remembering William and Ben and wanting to lay the blame somewhere for the goose needing to go. Uncle Charlie turned off the motorway on to quiet, country roads. Although they had set out early, it was dusk when they finally found a sign pointing the way to WESTIDE WILDFOWL SANCTUARY. A long, winding lane took them between fields and large exposed stretches of water. Josh recognized swans, ducks, geese and little moorhens, making their way like wind-up toys across the water.

"It's too quiet here," Josh pronounced, in a sulky voice.

"And that's the way the birds like it, I reckon," stated Uncle Charlie.

"None of them look injured to me," Josh

continued, knowing full well that nothing at the sanctuary would meet with his satisfaction.

"I expect the sanctuary attracts lots of wildfowl and birds. I doubt whether all of them are injured. After all, it is open to the sky," commented Uncle Charlie, trying to sound enthusiastic. "Apparently, the seriously sick or injured ones are cared for in pens close to the house. Look! If I'm not mistaken, it's just coming in to view," he said, with a sigh of relief, pleased to have reached the end of the journey.

Josh and his uncle were welcomed into the house by a lady with a warm smile on her weather-tanned face. They spent a few minutes in a small office. Its walls were covered in photographs and drawings of different birds and wildfowl, pictured with the people who had, presumably, rescued them. Large charts depicted the many species of wildfowl. Josh instantly recognized an illustration of a Canada Goose at the top of one chart. He stood studying the facts next to it while the lady fetched her son from the pens, where he

87

had been dispensing food to the casualties. Her son seemed friendly. He suggested that Uncle Charlie and Josh might like to help take the goose straight to one of the pens. He felt it would be a good idea to keep him there for a couple of days, while they observed him, before introducing him to the lakes.

Once inside his pen, with its own little wooden sleeping area and run, the goose waddled around making an inspection, before returning to Josh, who sat by the wire.

"He will be all right, won't he?" Josh anxiously asked the lady. "I mean – he'll soon settle in?"

The lady reassured Josh that everything would be done to help the goose return to a more natural habitat and way of life. Although he wouldn't fly again, he could still live close to the water: swimming, and feeding on it among other waterfowl. Josh gave the goose a final stroke on his head, before running to the van to hide the sad feelings that had welled up inside him. The goose clacked his beak and stared after Josh.

Josh hardly spoke a word throughout the

long journey home. In his nostrils he could smell the goose's own sharp odour. It was on his hands, too. Uncle Charlie tried to cheer him up by stopping at the service area on the motorway and treating them both to a huge plate of chips, sausages and beans. Josh was hungry, but he ate slowly and mechanically, gazing down at his plate until it was clean. He thanked Uncle Charlie, but didn't make an attempt to talk to him. His uncle understood how his nephew was feeling; he knew it would take some time for the boy to get over the goose going away. When Josh had finished his main meal, Uncle Charlie took the plate and replaced it with a large milkshake and a chunk of chocolate cake. Josh continued to eat in silence.

With a full stomach, Josh slept for the remainder of the journey home. Uncle Charlie had to tug at his nephew's sleeve to wake him, when they finally reached home. The boy struggled from the van and, accompanied by his uncle, plodded down the front path, in a daze like a sleepwalker. As Josh sat slumped on the edge of his bed and dragged off his clothes, a single grey feather floated to the floor. He bent to pick it up and studied it for a few minutes, realizing how beautifully it was formed, before placing it safely inside his jacket pocket. He lay on his bed and stared up at the ceiling, picturing the goose alone in his pen at the sanctuary. Shutting his eyes tight to block out the scene, Josh was soon overcome with tiredness and drifted off to sleep, wondering whether the creature had already forgotten him.

Chapter 13

Josh pottered around his uncle's house for the remaining few days of his holiday. Uncle Charlie was aware that his nephew's concern for the goose wasn't fading. One afternoon, Josh produced a sudden burst of energy and, to his uncle's amazement, decided to clean out the shed, disposing of any old straw the goose had used. He approached the chore furiously, as though ridding himself of his bitterness at losing a friend. Uncle Charlie was proud of him; he knew it was Josh's way of facing up to the fact that the goose had gone.

Josh accepted the offer of a fishing trip from Uncle Charlie one morning, but more to please his uncle than himself. Towards the end of the day, spent on a river bank, Uncle Charlie noticed that some of Josh's old enthusiasm had returned. In the evening, he suggested Josh might like to telephone the wildfowl sanctuary, because he felt the boy was adapting to the goose's absence. There was no need for Josh to feel completely cut off from any further contact, or news of him. He had, after all, played a big part in saving the goose and making him well again. Thinking back to recent, unfortunate incidents involving the creature, Uncle Charlie realized just how good a job Josh had made of giving the goose back a zest for life.

Josh was pleased when the lady at the sanctuary told him that the goose was faring well. Both she and her son had observed him and seen how well he coped with the damaged wing. In fact, he had proved too active to keep in the pen any longer, and was due to be released on to one of the lakes the following day.

Josh lay in bed that night, letting his imagination carry him over the miles to be reunited with the goose. This time, when he pictured him, he imagined the beautiful creature take to the water and, despite the trailing wing, glide over the surface. He could visualize the goose's long, thin neck held upright, his eyes fixed with a confident gleam as he sailed along like a stately galleon.

Josh rang the sanctuary several times in the first week. There was very little to report on each occasion; the goose was now living near the water, no doubt pleased to have gained his freedom again. The lady recognized the signs of a child who, despite putting on a brave face, was still obviously missing a very special creature in his life. She had seen it happen many times and suggested Josh should visit the sanctuary later in the year. Once again, Josh wondered if the goose had forgotten him – the boy who had stroked his head in the evenings to send him to sleep.

Chapter 14

Just as the lady had reported, the goose had been successfully released on the lake nearest the house. The lady and her son were satisfied he was in good health. A light dusting of feathers was just beginning to return around the site of the injury and he had continued to gain weight, the result of the careful feeding started by Josh.

A large cage had conveyed the goose to the water's edge. Without hesitation he had stepped out of it and waddled towards the lake, dipping his beak in among the weeds before paddling, with caution, in the shallows. The goose was inquisitive; he hadn't been in water for some time. He had looked about him, turning his head at the slightest sound. A mother duck and her brood of tiny, fluffy ducklings had seen him and altered course to make a quick inspection of the new arrival. But when he'd given her his beak-clacking welcome, she'd turned around and, gathering her babies close to her, led them squeaking their way back across the lake.

The clockwork motion of a moorhen had caught the goose's attention when it, too, suddenly appeared to be aiming straight for him. Then, as though remembering an urgent errand, the little creature had made a sharp detour, heading off in another direction. Two mallards had landed in the middle of the lake, in perfect water-skiing style: wide, rubbery feet skimming the surface, and bodies slowly lowered to meet the water. They had landed without causing as much as a ripple, but their loud, echoing quacks soon announced their arrival. They too had seen the goose, but had shown no interest in him.

As though aware of the limitations his injury imposed, the goose had glided cautiously along the edge of the lake where it was shallow, so that he could, if necessary, stand up. He had enjoyed feeling water beneath him. It was cool and gave off earthy smells, awakening his instincts to recall the waters where he'd been born. At one point, quite by accident, he'd sailed into a gathering of ducks hidden among some reeds. Startled by his presence they had lunged at him, quacking angrily and driving him away.

Having fed himself well from the rich waters, he had then decided to find a place to sleep. The sky and the temperature had indicated dusk was approaching. On one side of the lake there was a group of little wooden jetties where reeds and other water plants had sprung up. The goose had headed for them and, having made a quick inspection, decided upon one area in particular. It was well hidden, with soft, damp grass.

To the sounds of birds calling their last messages of the day, the goose had lowered and settled his body into the new resting place. As the sky had lost any trace of light and turned into a navy blue blanket over the earth, he had lain his head along his back,

drawing warmth to it from his body. Heavy lids had closed over his eyes and shut out the first day on the waters of his new home.

Chapter 15

A loud clap of thunder announced the beginning of another day. It was immediately followed by heavy rain. Several days had passed since the goose had been introduced to the lake and its inhabitants; still, none of them seemed particularly interested in the newcomer. While the rain pounded the surface of the water, most of the birds and waterfowl lay in the warmth of their nests around the lakes. From his bed among the reeds the goose observed only one creature moving over the wide expanse of water. As usual, it was a lone moorhen, scurrying across the lake on seemingly urgent business.

The goose looked down at the raindrops as

they slid off his waterproof feathers. He felt hungry and considered venturing a little way on to the lake to feed. Before setting out, he stretched his injured wing. It had become stiff, but he managed to produce an awkward flapping movement. Having carefully exercised it, he drew the wing to his side again, and moved out on to the water.

The heavy downpour had begun to slacken and turn to fine drizzle. The goose headed towards the centre of the lake, where there was a little island with a small hut and a few perches. Dipping his beak into the water, where it was deeper and coloured a rich, dark green, he fed greedily. When he was satisfied and refreshed, he preened himself. The pointed black beak dived into his plumage, nuzzling his feathers into order. Carried away by his activity, he'd been unaware of two other Canada geese who had swum up for a closer inspection of him. He greeted them with his friendly beak-clacking welcome, but they remained unmoved by the gesture, staring at him as though he was of no real significance. Did they see him as a threat? Did his trailing wing set him apart from their apparently perfect adult plumage? The two geese swam away, without as much as a backwards glance. The goose felt very lonely.

The rest of the day passed slowly. He cruised on the lake, but not even a busy moorhen paid him any attention.

He fed again, cleaned himself once more and, for want of something to do before returning to his patch to sleep, took to the banks. They were thick with mud caused by the morning rain. His wide, flat feet slapped up and down in the thick ooze, at one point sinking quite deep. For a moment his heart raced, as he struggled before successfully freeing them from the slimy mud. It clung thickly to his legs and feet. Wandering up the grassy bank, the goose felt the breeze changing to a strong wind. Heading into the oncoming wind, he experienced a sudden desire to take to the air as it blew between his feathers and reminded him of his last flight. How wonderful it would be to leave the friendless lake, take off – and fly.

The wind had gained strength and the

goose urged his muddy legs into a lumbering run, at the same time willing himself to lift off. Prior to his accident, he had made his take-offs from the water. Now on land, he directed all his energy into gaining enough speed to raise himself from the ground. His good wing began to move, its muscles, feathers and fibres crying out to lift him to the freedom of the skies. First one foot, then the other, bounded and leapt along the ground, until both were skimming just above it. The good wing was lifting him, but the other – the damaged one – refused to co-operate, still trailing uselessly by his side, and making a mockery of his attempt to fly. But for one exhilarating moment, he had experienced flight. It didn't matter about his haphazard style of flying – he had left the earth!

The crash-landing caused by the effort of trying to stay airborne resembled a child's kite falling to the ground. Stunned for a while, the goose flapped and fluttered in a heap on the soft grass, one wing splayed out at his side, sending messages of pain along its length. Eventually, exhausted by his efforts,

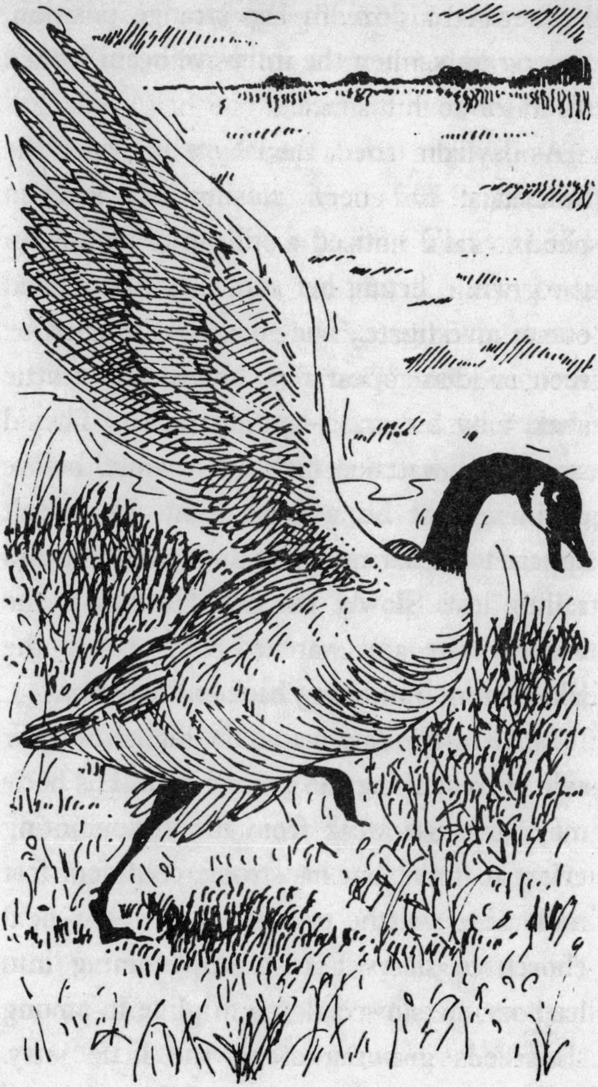

he began to doze in the strange position, waking only when the intrusive beam from a torch shone in his face.

As daylight faded, the lady who owned the sanctuary had been closing her kitchen blinds. She'd noticed a still, grey bundle on the grass. Alerting her son, they had rushed out to investigate. The goose was startled by their sudden appearance; he was still a little shaken by his crash–landing earlier. They'd stood and watched him for a while, before deciding that he was all right. He didn't appear to be harmed, just uncomfortable and a little lost. Slowly, the lady led him to the water's edge and watched him take to the lake, before wandering back to the house.

Entering the dark water, the night's chill air sent shivers along the goose's back. His body may have felt weak from his disappointing effort at flight, but his strong, confident feet took him swiftly to the spot where he'd chosen to sleep. Like a ship coming into harbour, he slowed down to glide in among the reeds growing along the little jetty. Lifting one foot, ready to feel the soft grass beneath it, he became aware of a violent hissing among the maze of reeds and grasses. A blow from a mighty wing suddenly sent him off balance. Terrified, the goose backed clumsily out of the reeds and on to the water again. He was stunned and fearful. The creature who'd delivered the blow appeared in an instant, looming above him, hissing, spitting and lashing out with its powerful golden beak. Both of its wings were raised in readiness to come down with force on the poor goose. Petrified, he stared up at them, as they blocked out the moonlight, like a great cloak. A swan – and a vicious one – fanned the air with its majestic, pure white wings and rose on its legs to make itself appear even more imposing. The goose cowered, backing away from the draught caused by the swan's beating wings.

From the relative safety of the bank, the goose watched the swan return to his resting place. No creature on the lake would dare challenge its power; it could choose exactly where it would sleep and feed.

The lake fell silent once again, and the sky

appeared to be empty of stars. The goose lay down on the bank, unable to decide whether to find another place to sleep, or to stay put. Exhausted by his earlier efforts, he eventually fell asleep.

Chapter 16

Soft, early-morning light fell on the goose's sleeping form. On waking, he saw how close he still lay to the resting place from which he'd been so viciously evicted the previous night. He decided to take to the water and head across the lake to the other side. Through the swirling mist suspended over the water, he saw the little island looming up; he could break his journey. As he paddled up its narrow shore the raucous quacks from ducks, annoyed by their early morning visitor, was the only greeting he received. The angry creatures had shown their annoyance, until their chorus seemed to tell the goose to go away.

Reaching the other side of the lake he found a few straggly trees, their branches bent low to the water, some dipping below the surface. Only two ducks rested beneath them. They lifted their heads at his approach, but showed no further interest. As the goose settled on the bank, high above him he could hear the familiar "AARGH-HONK" of two Canada geese in flight. Longing to join them, he watched them until their cries faded.

He ate little that day and began to lose interest in any kind of activity. It seemed to him that wherever he went, his company just wasn't acceptable. Through sad eyes the goose watched the morning sky lighten, while the mist lifted from the lake. In the distance, the familiar sound of an old van, like Uncle Charlie's, rattled along the drive to the house. But before he was up on his feet and moving in its direction, the vehicle, a delivery van, had performed its task and was off down the drive. It soon disappeared into the distance, but the goose remained for several minutes, waiting expectantly.

Later that morning he watched while

another two geese were introduced to the water by the lady and her son. One goose limped badly, due to a deformed foot. The other possessed hardly any feathers on one side of its body. Both took to the water, staying close to each other, and swam away to a patch of tall grasses, where they appeared to settle with ease. Once again, he felt out of place at the sanctuary. The lakes had everything he needed to sustain a comfortable life: lots of water, plenty of food, and the freedom to move around. But the goose had sensed the atmosphere to be both friendless and hostile since his encounter with the swan.

It was another chance meeting with the swan, who appeared to recognize him from the previous night, that made the goose want to run away. He noticed the impressive, elegant creature as it glided gracefully across the lake to the island. There was something very regal about the way it sailed through the water, that made other birds move aside to let it pass. The goose watched the swan's magnificent head turn from side to side, surveying the lake. The creature was very beautiful, but its beauty masked anger. Suddenly, it seemed to sense the goose's presence beneath the trees. First, the long white neck and stately head turned to face him, then the rest of its body shifted position to follow as it aimed directly towards the bank. Like a warship heading for an enemy target, the swan moved swiftly and accurately across the water – it was aiming straight for the goose. As though hypnotized, the poor goose stayed rooted to the spot. But he wasn't being brave; he knew he would be unable to compete with the swan's strength. What compelled him to stare at the creature so brazenly was the sight of one of its wings, which had begun to trail, just like his own damaged wing. Fascinated by his observation, he just kept staring, right up until the moment the swan rose from the water in front of him. With its neck thrust out, using its powerful, golden beak, it pecked at the soft, young plumage on the goose's chest. Flustered and afraid, he took to his feet and fled towards the far lake. The swan pursued him, nipping at his tail feathers as the goose zigzagged his way across the grass.

He carried on running, even after the swan had given up the chase. Exhausted, he eventually stopped to turn around. The swan had sunk down on to the grass; it was bothered by the awkward wing. Obviously distressed, the elegant creature pecked at the feathers, trying to urge the wing back to its side. Eventually, it gave up on the task and lay resting; all pursuit of the goose had slipped from its mind. While the swan dozed, the goose made his way back to the lake, putting plenty of distance between himself and his assailant. He drank greedily from the green water to refresh himself, before paddling to a clump of unoccupied reeds to hide.

Chapter 17

Most of the birds and wildfowl had settled themselves for the night. Ducklings had jostled one another for a better position beneath their mother's wings, and geese had arranged their sleeping quarters before lowering their large bodies on top of sturdy, but spindly, legs. The only creature swimming on the lake was a moorhen. She was making an erratic search for her chick, whose squeaks she followed. The goose looked around: everything appeared to be so peaceful. He was tired and as activity around the water died down, he too began to feel the need to rest. But the sudden sound of a goose hissing, not too far away, soon made him recall the vicious swan, and his instinct to survive was sharpened. He had to move away – return to safety.

Leaving the side of the lake, he headed in the opposite direction to the house. The waters and land of the sanctuary were bordered by a high, wire fence. Keeping his head low, he moved along the fence, feeling the level of the ground with his beak, until a slight dip in the earth presented itself. By tugging at the grass and digging with his beak, he was able to create a hole, just big enough for him to squeeze through. His tunnelling activities soon met with success, but not without pain. Dragging the injured wing beneath the wire hurt him, especially when some of the feathers became caught. Undaunted, he tugged and pulled the wing through, leaving a clump of soft plumage clinging to the wire. It didn't bother him – he was free. Soon he built up a steady pace which took him into the distance.

The sky was turning a velvety black when the goose chose to rest; his legs were exhausted. The grass was long, and close by there were a few trees providing shelter from a crisp wind which had started to blow. On tired legs, he slowly eased himself down and folded himself into his wings for warmth. The sleep, which soon enveloped him, gave rest and strength to his body.

The goose was woken, early the next morning, by the sound of birds singing. He looked up at the powdery, blue sky, then at the fields which stretched to the horizon on all sides. He stood for while, flexing both wings and nuzzling the ground with his beak to draw moisture from the damp grass. Moving off, once again keeping in a straight line, he sensed movement as he disturbed the grass with his wide, flat feet. Rabbits scurried to their burrows and insects scuttled along thin blades of grass, which bent low beneath the weight of the tiny creatures when they reached the tip. The goose sensed his freedom; it gave purpose to his stride. He trusted his instincts to lead him back to the place where he wanted to be most of all.

A strong, sweet smell of hay reached him as he hopped and fluttered through a broken wooden gate into a field where cattle fed. Turning their munching jaws in his direction, they watched while the intruder crossed their land. They were not in the least bothered by his presence, even when he availed himself of their drinking water, which slopped over the edges of an old tin bath. The goose dipped his beak in it, held his head up and let the cool water trickle down his throat to refresh him – it tasted good.

"AARGH-HONK, AARGH-HONK!" he called, expressing the sheer pleasure the water, his surroundings, and freedom gave him. The cattle looked up at the sound and, for a moment, stood rigid, apart from their jaws, which continued to swivel as they chewed. Then, lowering their heavy heads to the sweet grass, they returned to their grazing. The field provided the goose with his first meal of the day. At one end, to one side, a small duck pond was presided over by one little, snow-white duck. The pond proved to be full of all the nutrients the goose needed to sustain him for a while. He sank his beak down into its earthy, brown depths, while the little duck cruised cautiously along the bank, observing him. When the goose raised his head to stare at the little creature, she sensed he meant her no harm and, satisfied that he wouldn't chase her away, stayed close by.

The goose lay down to clean his feathers, pecking at his plumage, before moving off. Refreshed and ready to continue his quest, he set off across the field, escorted for a short distance by the inquisitive, snow-white duck. The next field contained a farmhouse. The goose paused at the sound of machinery whirring and a dog barking in deep, hoarse tones. Hidden by the long grass, shaded by overhanging trees, the goose made his way across the field which stretched far into the distance.

Night-time found him at the edge of a vast wood. The fields ended abruptly in a barrier of thick trees. Woodland night-sounds seemed strange to him: some made him afraid and he found it difficult to settle. Fluffing up his feathers to warm his body, he turned his head at the sound of a fox barking. Soon the eerie hoots of an owl added to his fear, and made him even more restless. He had heard these sounds before, but not alone, and from the confines of a wood. The trees served to amplify the sound. Although his eyes ached to close, part of him refused to sleep, staying alert and at the ready in case he should need to run. Eventually, exhaustion overtook him and he fell into a deep sleep.

During the night a young fox caught the goose's scent and followed his well-developed sense of smell to where the creature lay. The fox had never tackled the appetizing proportions of a goose before; not even a young one. He prowled up and down, working out his best angle of attack, excited, but also apprehensive. The goose stirred in his sleep, then suddenly awoke to see the fox close by. Immediately, the goose uncoiled his neck and, holding it as straight as an arrow, lashed out at the surprised creature. In the same manner as he had alarmed Uncle Charlie among the reeds, he spat and hissed, raising his strong wing to make him look bigger. The young fox leapt backwards, but didn't run off; the goose had smelled too delicious to give up on. He was hungry and he licked his lips in anticipation of securing his tasty-looking prey. Up and down he paced, hoping to get an advantage over the goose from a different angle. But the goose stayed alert and moved his head, following the fox's movements. When the persistent predator came too near, the goose became indignant and bold. Flapping his good wing, his heart pounding within his soft chest, he rushed head on at the fox and scared him. Still the animal refused to give up. He slid away to rest among some bushes, and lay low to consider any further move he might make on the brave goose. He hoped the goose would soon tire and, in an unguarded moment, the delicious-scented prize would be his.

The goose was as determined to fend off the fox's attack as the fox was set on acquiring the goose. And the fox's patience was almost rewarded, when, for a second, the goose bent his head to peck at an irritation in his injured wing. It was just long enough to give the fox a chance to bring him down. The crafty young

predator seized his opportunity – he was up and running towards the goose once more.

But the fox had underestimated the speed of the goose. As the fox sprang, the goose aimed his beak like a sword at the animal's side, where it made contact with soft flesh. The fox yelped and fell, tumbling on the earthy floor. Before he had a chance to stand, the goose lunged at him once more, pecking at the fox's neck and bringing his good wing down hard on the startled creature. Their roles had changed; the goose had become the attacker. Not a drop of blood was drawn, but the young fox felt bruised where the sharp beak had jabbed repeatedly at him. With his tail hanging low, he eventually loped off among the trees; all hope of securing his meal had vanished from his thoughts. He turned, only once, to stare at the goose, disappointed that he'd failed to triumph. He certainly hadn't expected the creature to put up such a fight. That night, the fox would have to make do with smaller prey for his meal. The goose was exhausted after his amazing display of courage. But he sensed that where he had encountered one fox, it was likely there would be others. Because of this, he dozed fitfully throughout the night, only too aware of the slightest rustle in the bushes.

With the arrival of the dawn, pale sunlight penetrated the thick foliage of the tall trees. It also revealed the vastness of the woods. The goose was still tired and longed to sense more sky above him, great patches of it. The sky made him feel safer. Hungry, he staggered to his feet, ruffled his feathers and set off through the woodland.

Several hours passed before the trees began to thin out. He became aware of larger patches of blue sky between the treetops. This spurred him on to a point where the woods ended abruptly, marked by a high, rustic fence. Unlike the fence at the sanctuary, which was well constructed, this one didn't require the goose to dig his way out. He found a gap and squeezed through. Immediately on the other side lay a steep, grassy bank. As the goose climbed it, he became aware of a low humming noise. When he reached the top, the noise had changed to a loud roar – and he was confronted by several lanes of fast-moving traffic.

Chapter 18

Uncle Charlie had assembled all that was necessary for a quiet, restful evening. Within arm's reach was his meal, a newspaper, and a fishing magazine. His fork sank easily into a mound of soft, fluffy mashed potato that accompanied a large helping of stew and a pile of peas. He had to confess to himself that he missed his nephew; even the poor goose at times. But he felt confident that, sad though it was for Josh, the goose was settled in the best possible place. Life could resume its predictably comfortable routine.

William and Ben had become the best of friends. To Uncle Charlie's annoyance, they often conducted conversations with one another across his garden while he was working there. He felt as though he was invisible on these occasions. The keen gardeners, who had once detested one another, were now united against him. They still remembered, with bitterness, the events that had, strangely enough, brought them together.

The stew had tasted good; now the rhubarb crumble and thick custard provided another interesting challenge for Uncle Charlie's taste buds. Just as he liked it: the rhubarb had little sugar. Its sharp taste made him pucker his lips. Uncle Charlie's meal drew to a close as the six o'clock news was also coming to an end. He scooped up the last delicious spoonful of custard and was just about to savour it, when the concluding news item caught his attention.

"And finally," the newscaster said, "a goose brought traffic to a standstill on the M3 motorway today. An eight-mile tailback of vehicles was unable to proceed, due to a young Canada goose with an injured wing. The goose successfully dodged cars and lorries as it headed for the central reservation, where it rested before losing itself among the traffic. Police contacted experts from a wild-fowl sanctuary, where it is believed to have resided, but all attempts to capture it have, so far, failed. A further update on the 'goose on the run' will be given on the nine o'clock news."

Uncle Charlie's last spoonful of custard never made it to his mouth, which stayed wide open throughout the newscaster's words. Accompanying the announcement was film of a grey Canada goose which he felt sure he recognized as the recent resident at his home. The report showed the poor creature squatting and cowering on the grassy reserva-tion area between lanes of traffic. Uncle Charlie had hardly found time to push his dish away, when the telephone rang. A breathless Josh shouted down the receiver:

"Did you see him, Uncle? Did you see *our goose* on the news? I know it's him – I'd know him *anywhere*. We've got to save him! He looks terrified. Shall we go there, *now*?"

Uncle Charlie had experienced the strangest feeling, while driving home from the sanctuary, that he hadn't seen the last of the unfortunate goose, who through no fault of his own seemed to have become involved in the busy world that humans inhabited. He tried to calm his nephew by telling him that there was little they could do so far away from the incident. They could only await the next news report and try not to get flustered. Uncle Charlie said he felt sure the police would soon have the matter in hand and return the goose safely to the sanctuary. Josh was quick to reply that he wondered why the goose had left in the first place.

Indigestion had Uncle Charlie bound to his chair until the nine o'clock news. When it came, there was further cause for concern. Continued failure to catch the goose had resulted in it escaping the terrifying ordeal of the motorway, by fleeing beneath the stationary wheels of several huge trucks, to reach the bank on the other side of the traffic. Still pursued by police and the sanctuary owners, he'd taken to the fields, squeezing beneath fences and hiding in long grass, until reaching a wide expanse of water. Using searchlights, the police had finally tracked him down on the water, far enough away from being a threat to the motorway traffic. The lady from the wildfowl sanctuary had announced it was best if she, and a few others, remained in an attempt to recapture him in the morning.

The exhausted goose was glad to be on water again, able to drink, feed and revive his aching body. The powerful beam trained on him from time to time disturbed him. He needed to be on his way.

In the early hours of the morning, when thick mist shrouded the edges of the water, the goose slipped away unseen by his pursuers. Suddenly realizing his absence, the watchers went in search of him among the reeds. But the goose was on the move – "on the run" – once more. Slipping beneath hedges, fluttering through fences, he was soon so deeply immersed in the landscape that it was impossible for his pursuers to detect him. Within a few hours, they called off the search.

At home, Josh hardly slept for worrying about the goose. Uncle Charlie found it hard to find peace from his nephew's constant pleas to go off in search of him. He had telephoned the wildfowl sanctuary and learned that there was little to be done. They had seen no evidence to show the goose hadn't settled with them during his stay and were very surprised that he'd gone. The lady said that if he didn't show up again, it was probably because he'd found somewhere more to his taste. Uncle Charlie hoped that was the situation – just so long as the goose was well and safe. Josh wasn't so sure; he wanted the goose where he could see that he was safe, preferably right in front of him. He tried hard not to pester his uncle to go off in search of the goose, but found it hard to contain his impatience for more news.

Chapter 19

Two days after the news item, Uncle Charlie pulled his newspaper from the letterbox and, through sleepy eyes, focused on a large front page photograph of a goose sitting on the runway of a small aerodrome. Above the picture was the caption, "RUNAWAY GOOSE TURNS UP ON THE RUNWAY!" The article went on to say how the goose the nation had seen holding up traffic only days before had now presented itself at a small aerodrome used by several flying clubs. He had first been spotted by the man in the control tower who'd reported to all pilots already in the air that a goose was squatting on the landing strip. It would need to be removed before they had clearance to land. Only minutes later, several flight instructors had attempted to catch the goose but, yet again, he'd managed to resist capture. Fleeing across the airfields, he had then found his way on to more farmland. The man in the control tower had reached for his camera and taken several photographs of the goose before it escaped. A national newspaper had been only too delighted to print them.

The minute Uncle Charlie finished reading the story, the telephone rang – he knew it would be Josh. His nephew had seen the picture of the goose and was distraught. Uncle Charlie decided to contact the newspaper and tell them all he knew about the poor creature. The newspaper's editor was very pleased to hear from him; the story had the kind of appeal that sold newspapers. He would print a contact number and address, for readers who thought they had seen the goose. Uncle Charlie could then decide whether to follow up any likely sightings.

Josh and Uncle Charlie posed for the newspaper photographer later that day. Josh found the sudden interest in him exciting, but at the back of his mind he was concerned for the goose's safety. Uncle Charlie resigned himself to the fact that there would be no peace for his nephew, and very little for himself, until the goose was, once again, at home in the den.

Many people in the country took news-papers from their letterboxes the next morning, and saw a large photograph of Uncle Charlie and Josh on the front page. Below it, a caption proclaimed: "GOOSE ON THE RUN HAS FRIENDS IN THE SOUTH."

Uncle Charlie was amazed to read how: "Retired bachelor Charlie, with the help of his nephew, Josh, performed a daring rescue of the young goose some weeks ago. They snatched it from certain death on a pond, while out fishing." The article went on to relate how they had cared for the goose until it was necessary to take him to the sanctuary.

At his school, Josh was treated like a celebrity. He was invited by the headmistress to stand up in assembly and tell the pupils all about his adventure with the goose. Josh did as he was asked, but his heart wasn't in it; he just wanted his friend safely home again.

Hundreds of calls, many of them hoaxes, were taken by the newspaper's offices. All claimed, within hours of the article appearing, to have seen the goose. Some people even rang in from as far away as Scotland. Uncle Charlie was sure they had all seen some sort of goose, but not necessarily *the* goose. A pile of mail had also arrived at the newspaper's offices to be delivered to Uncle Charlie's house, for him to sift through.

In the following week he found himself opening his front door either to other newspaper reporters, who'd tracked him down, or to nosey neighbours caught up in the excitement of having a newsworthy person living only a few doors away. But Uncle Charlie still found time to sit in his kitchen and telephone some of the numbers he had been given. Many were excited children who, when asked about the goose, either claimed that it had flown away, or described a creature bearing little resemblance to a Canada goose. There were also letters from wildfowl experts offering advice on recapture, and from sympathetic people who had owned geese which had either run away or died.

To his horror, towards the end of the week, Uncle Charlie opened a letter from a lady who'd seen his photograph in the newspaper. She lived alone on a farm, apart from several geese, and felt that she and Uncle Charlie could strike up a friendship, considering they shared a common interest in geese. The lady hoped he would soon pay her a visit. Uncle Charlie's face turned deathly pale as he thrust the letter away from him.

Turning to a particularly grubby envelope and tearing it open, he gasped as he lifted out a photograph of a goose cowering in the doorway of a run-down farm building. He reached for his glasses and scrutinized the picture. Unless he was very much mistaken, he could even make out a few splodges of the gloss paint, still visible on the goose's plumage, remaining from his rampage in the den. The poor creature looked dirty and neglected, but Uncle Charlie felt convinced it was the right goose. There was no letter accompanying the photograph, only some words scrawled untidily on the back of the picture: "I will 'phone you at 7.00p.m. Thursday. Be in – if you want to see your goose alive again!"

Uncle Charlie felt cold. This was no hoax – and it was Thursday. He didn't bother with the rest of the letters or contact numbers. It would be difficult, but he had to keep his discovery from Josh; the boy would only become frantic with worry if he knew. Uncle Charlie examined the envelope again. He tried hard to decipher the postmark, but failed. On a map, he marked in pencil the places where the goose had been sighted. To his amazement, despite its route straying a little, the goose had been heading in the right direction for his home.

Although Uncle Charlie had been awaiting the call at seven o'clock, the sudden ringing made him jump. He grabbed the receiver. There was silence, for a moment, at the other end, then a gruff, unpleasant-sounding voice spoke. "I take it you have my little package by now?" Uncle Charlie replied that he'd received a photograph of a badly neglected goose. The man laughed, mocking the note of concern in Uncle Charlie's voice.

"Well, I'll get straight to the point. If you want to see your precious goose – ever again – then I want four thousand pounds by tomorrow evening!" He gave Uncle Charlie an address and brief directions of how to get there, strongly advising him not to disclose the details to anyone, especially the police. The slightest suspicion that they had been informed of the goose's whereabouts would ensure an end of the matter – and of the goose. Uncle Charlie entreated the man at least to give the goose some water and a little food. He replied, "Listen, if that thing's stupid enough to walk right into my kitchen and start pecking up crumbs, I reckon I *have* fed him!" The man laughed again, ignoring any further pleas Uncle Charlie made to treat the goose well by slamming down the receiver.

Quite by chance, the goose had come upon the man's farmhouse and its shabby out-buildings after scrambling through a hedge. Hunger and thirst had led him to the kitchen door. Wandering into the messy, deserted room, he had found a dog's bowl, brimful with fresh water, and drunk thirstily from it. Crumbs on the dirty floor had provided the goose with a little nourishment. While he had been foraging for the morsels, a savage dog had suddenly appeared in the doorway. It was soon to be joined by its master, who restrained the dog from attacking the goose, realizing it was possible that the creature was the very same goose featured in the newspapers. What luck! It had walked right into his kitchen. Studying the goose's photograph, the man felt sure he had the right goose; the trailing wing confirmed it. The "Goose on the Run" was definitely on his premises – and he could profit from his feathered visitor.

With the assistance of his dog the man hadn't found it too difficult to drive the terrified goose into one of the cold, dirty outbuildings. Pausing just long enough to take a quick photograph of him, the man had shut the goose in without food or water. In a nearby town the photograph was rapidly developed and the ransom demand written on the back to be posted to the newspaper's contact number for Uncle Charlie.

Uncle Charlie found it hard to sleep. The matter of the goose drifted round and round in his mind like a thunder cloud. By morning, he had resolved that there really was no way to save the poor creature, other than by meeting the man's unfair demand.

The bank opened soon after Uncle Charlie arrived to withdraw the required amount from his account. It made him sad to think the ransom money would take all his savings. He hesitated for a moment, holding the notes tightly in his hand, before recalling the tone of the man's voice on the telephone; he was undoubtedly a villain. If the goose was to be saved, the man's demand had to be met.

Before he left, Uncle Charlie telephoned Josh to say he would be out until late that evening. Armed with little more than a flask of tea and a chunk of cake for the journey, he set off to find the man and, it was to be hoped, retrieve the goose.

Chapter 20

The old van seemed to sense the urgency of the mission, performing as if it was still the bright, shining vehicle Uncle Charlie had purchased long ago. He had continued to breathe life into it throughout the many years it had occupied his driveway, and now it was needed for another vital mission. Uncle Charlie seemed oblivious to the symphony of rattles and squeaks coming from the van's bodywork.

Hours later, in a long, winding country lane, he pulled up to consult his map. The address of the farm the man had given him was only a matter of a few miles from a large town. But the back roads leading to it proved to be a maze of high hedges, with few signposts. He felt sure he had driven through most of the main lanes several times, without seeing any indication of the farm he sought. Passing a little village post office for the second time, he considered stopping to enquire if they knew of the address. But he recalled the man's words and changed his mind. Perhaps it was better not to draw any attention to his quest until he had the goose safely in his hands.

On the outskirts of the village, he decided to take a right turn through a dark, deeply-hedged lane. A rusty old sign that had come loose from one of its hinges creaked in the wind. Uncle Charlie pulled up to inspect it. A closer look revealed he had found the farm. Drawing a deep breath, he turned the van on to a rough, narrow track leading to a cluster of old farm buildings. The van's brakes squeaked to a halt in the yard, announcing Uncle Charlie's arrival.

The place looked derelict. From the shambles that formed one of the outbuildings, a thin, muddy cow ambled across the farmyard towards a trough, half-filled with stagnant water. The animal's ribs protruded from sunken, scrawny sides. It paused to look round at the van, raising its head to issue a feeble "Moo!" Uncle Charlie was both saddened and angered by its condition. At one end of the yard, a few scraggy-looking chickens pecked the ground, desperate for food which was nowhere to be found. Uncle Charlie soon became aware of several other animals. Apart from the cow and the chickens, there was a thin black mother cat with two sickly-looking kittens, who occupied a discarded box by the side of another outbuilding. A goat stood tethered to a post. The animal was trying hard to reach a few dry thistles growing from a wall.

Even before the owner of the sad little collection of neglected creatures appeared, Uncle Charlie was bubbling with rage at their plight. He checked himself for a moment: what if the owner was ill and incapable of looking after himself and his animals? Perhaps, in kidnapping the goose, he'd seen a way to provide for them all. Such a situation was instantly dismissed from Uncle Charlie's mind when the owner emerged from his gloomy farmhouse kitchen. Uncle Charlie had imagined the owner of the voice he had heard on the telephone to be bigger and older. The man who strode towards him was thin with quick, shifting eyes. His clothes were shabby and dirty and, at his side, a heavy, muscular dog bared its teeth, tugging impatiently at its lead. Compared with the other animals, it seemed well-fed and robust. The man kept pulling on its short lead, as though displaying to Uncle Charlie how he was forced to restrain it from attacking.

"Come for your little feathered friend, have you?" hissed the man. He leaned through the van's open window with a sneer on his unshaven face, while his dog clawed at the door. Uncle Charlie took an instant dislike to the menacing expression in the man's eyes.

"Are these *your* animals?" Uncle Charlie demanded to know, indicating with a sweeping glance the pathetic group of creatures in the yard.

"They're mine, all right. But what's that

got to do with you?" replied the man.

"I *care* about them, and that has everything to do with me. *Look* at them! They're half-starved and sick. You should be ashamed to keep them in such a state!" Uncle Charlie's face had turned red with anger. The man continued to smirk at him. Ignoring Uncle Charlie's criticism, he said,

"If you're here to talk business, then let's get *on* with it – I'm a busy man and you know what I want!"

"Only when you put that beast of yours inside the house – and lock it in!" Uncle Charlie demanded, only too aware of the dog, now standing on its hind legs and snarling in at the window of the van; its vile-smelling breath filling Uncle Charlie's nostrils.

The man laughed and untwisted his body from the awkward position he had adopted while leaning on the van. Uncle Charlie was reminded of a thin, poisonous snake un-coiling itself. Without saying another word, the man slouched across the yard with the dog, and did as Uncle Charlie had requested. With caution, Uncle Charlie got out of the van, noticing as he did so how cramped his legs felt from the long journey. The man was soon back at his visitor's side.

"I've got the money, but first, I want to see the goose," Uncle Charlie insisted defiantly, meeting the man's threatening stare.

With his mouth lifting at the corners, forming more of a grimace than a smile, the man indicated that Uncle Charlie should follow him towards an outhouse. Inside, the stench of years of neglect was overpowering and made Uncle Charlie's stomach feel queasy. It was difficult to make out the shape of anything in the gloom, but as his eyes became accustomed to the dark, the pitiable form of some sort of creature cowering in one corner of a filthy pen came into focus. It was the goose.

"Haven't you even left out water for the poor thing?" Uncle Charlie snapped. He could feel his temper rising again.

"*Look!*" the man said, pointing a grimy finger in Uncle Charlie's face. "If you want the thing, *take it*! But I want the money in my hand before I let you both leave this place."

Uncle Charlie entered the pen, knelt down and spoke softly to the goose, coaxing it from the corner. At the sound of his voice, the goose got to his feet and took several tentative steps towards him. The miserable creature waddled up and, appearing to recognize Uncle Charlie, rested his long, slim neck on his knee. He even managed to clack his beak to welcome him.

"Well, well!" the man exclaimed, sarcastically. "This is a very touching reunion, but as I said, I'm a busy man – so give me the money and take the wretched thing *away*!"

Uncle Charlie picked up the goose and started to head for his van, eager to get the stench of the place out of his nostrils. The man reacted quickly by stepping in front of him to bar his way:

"Not so fast! You must think I'm stupid. The goose stays here until I get my cash – just in case you're thinking of putting the thing in your van and driving off!"

"I just want to take him out into the fresh air. He's weak; he won't run off. I *promise* you," pleaded Uncle Charlie.

The man's face contorted into a mass of grimy wrinkles. Grudgingly, he agreed. Uncle Charlie put the goose down and proceeded to the van. The goose and the man followed close behind. Uncle Charlie reached inside the glove compartment and withdrew a fat envelope, stuffed full with his money. He revealed its contents to the man, advising him to spend some of it on food and shelter for his poor, starving animals. Motivated by the sight of so many banknotes, the man suddenly lunged towards Uncle Charlie, grabbing at the money with greedy, outstretched hands. Without warning, the goose, thinking the man was attacking Uncle Charlie, dashed straight at him. His neck was low and thrust out, his good wing raised high. Pecking and jabbing at the man's bony shins, the goose repeatedly attacked him. Uncle Charlie was speechless. When the horrible man tried to kick the goose away, the angry creature's attack became all the more frenzied.

"You're for it *now*!" the man shrieked, trying to escape the goose by running in the direction of the house. But the goose stayed close on his heels. "Just wait till I get my dog!" the man shouted. But to his dismay, he stumbled over a rut in the ground and scattered some of the notes. As they floated up into the hedge, he tried to retrieve them, but the goose continued to jab at his legs.

Uncle Charlie called to the goose, who took one last peck before running obediently back to his friend. Uncle Charlie lifted him and placed him, with speed, on to a blanket in the back of the van. Locking the door he then rushed to the driving seat, delighted to find the old vehicle responding surprisingly well to his speedy manoeuvres. Reversing down the long track, he swung the van on to the road and didn't stop until he reached the nearest town.

"*Clever* goose!" he shouted happily. Grubby, shabby and hungry after his ordeal, the goose still managed to respond with a contented clack of his beak. He was happy to be with Uncle Charlie once more.

Lifting the goose from the van with care, Uncle Charlie marched with him right into the police station at the nearby town.

"Hey, Sarge," the policeman at the desk called to his superior. "It's that goose in the papers and on the telly – you know? The one on the run!"

While the goose drank thirstily from a bowl of water, Uncle Charlie related his experiences at the farm, explaining why he'd been afraid to contact the police and had gone ahead in delivering the ransom. He was relieved to see two policemen sent to the farm in pursuit of the man. News of the ill treatment and neglect of the man's animals came as no surprise to the sergeant. The unpleasant character had been in trouble on many occasions, and warned about the dreadful conditions in which he kept his animals. Now they would be taken away from him to receive proper attention.

Uncle Charlie telephoned Josh to tell him the good news about the goose. His nephew was thrilled to hear that he was safe. Josh was also eager to hear all the exciting details of the rescue. Most of all, he demanded an explanation as to why he hadn't been allowed to accompany his uncle on the venture.

The goose slept all the way home. Uncle Charlie was exhausted when he pulled into his driveway much later that day. While the hungry goose gulped down his food in the kitchen, the dust and grime from his travels and adventures was cleaned away by Uncle Charlie. When the goose's stomach was full, he settled on an old blanket, watching every move Uncle Charlie made – almost afraid to let him out of his sight. Worn out from the day's events, Uncle Charlie slumped into his armchair and gazed at the goose, trying to imagine all that had befallen him since they'd parted at the sanctuary. Before Uncle Charlie had time to feed himself, he fell asleep. The goose also slept, but lightly; the slightest noise woke him. Whenever he opened his eyes, he was relieved to see familiar surroundings and Uncle Charlie snoring in his chair.

Chapter 21

The newspaper which had featured the goose's story was delighted by the latest turn of events. It seemed to Uncle Charlie that he had only just put the telephone down when a reporter and photographer from the newspaper were knocking on his door. Josh arrived at the same time, desperate to see the goose. Uncle Charlie related his story, while Josh knelt on the floor by the much-travelled creature, who was obviously excited to see the boy again. He clacked his beak and nuzzled the boy's hair. Josh fought back tears of happiness at their reunion, and stroked the goose's soft head, whispering to him, "You're safe now. *Nobody* will *ever* take you away from us again."

Wherever Josh went, the goose followed him. Seizing the opportunity for some good shots, the newspaper's photographer reeled off lots of film. Just as Uncle Charlie, Josh and the goose were posed for a group photograph, the telephone rang. Uncle Charlie answered it. Immediately his face broke into a broad smile. He had more good news: the police had apprehended the villain at the farm, just as he was about to leave on a long journey, taking only his dog and the money. The villain would face prosecution and his animals would be given good homes.

The next day, the newspaper carried the full story with a wonderful picture of Josh, Uncle Charlie and the goose. "GOOSE ON THE RUN COMES HOME TO ROOST!" the headline proclaimed. If Uncle Charlie thought the newspaper's report was the end of the matter – he was wrong. Several local papers, magazines and television crews wanted interviews with the celebrities. The road buzzed with excitement. Once more, inquisitive neighbours, anxious to get their faces on camera, stood on the doorstep. Even William and Ben put in an appearance, offering to let the television crew use their beautiful gardens as locations for any interviews. When Uncle Charlie informed them that the goose would naturally accompany him and Josh, both William and Ben swallowed hard. Forcing smiles, they retreated awkwardly.

When Uncle Charlie and Josh saw themselves and the goose featured on television later in the evening, they laughed out loud, remembering how the goose had pecked at the microphone the interviewer had held. Uncle Charlie kept repeating to himself, "Well, who would have thought it? *Us* on the six o'clock news."

With the excitement over for the day, Uncle Charlie lay in bed finding it difficult to sleep. Although he was so pleased that the goose was safe and his nephew had stopped worrying, his mind was racing ahead to a time when he would need to consider the goose's long-term future. It had already been proved how impossible it was to keep the creature confined on the allotment. Somewhere more permanent would still need to be found – but

where? He knew it would break his nephew's heart for the goose to be parted from him for a second time. Even if another home, better equipped for keeping the goose, was to be found, there would still be no guarantee that he would stay put. He was obviously only happy near Josh. There had to be a solution! For the present, the goose had returned, contentedly, to the den.

It came as a great surprise one morning when, after a stroll around the front and back gardens with the goose close on his heels, Uncle Charlie received a telephone call from an old friend he hadn't heard from in years. The man had seen an article about the goose, featuring a first-hand account by his old friend Charlie, who grinned out of a photograph at the reader. Uncle Charlie was thrilled to speak to the man again and was soon happily reminiscing over old times. But, caught up in the pleasure of the surprise call, he had broken one of his most important rules for the goose: he had left the side gate, leading to the front garden, wide open.

"My goodness!" he said, when he eventually put down the receiver, forty minutes later. "How time flies! Now, what *was* I doing before the 'phone rang?" He was trying to recall his actions when an insistent ringing on his doorbell distracted him. Opening the door with a bright smile upon his face, his expression changed rapidly, when he found himself confronted by a strange assortment of people on his doorstep. A large garden gnome with a broken nose, hat and fishing-rod was thrust up close to his face by an irate lady who lived a few doors away. Another neighbour clutched an enormous plastic flamingo. Its garishly-coloured beak hung in shreds and its head was twisted, so that one eye stared vacantly up at the sky. A total stranger pointed to the front wheel of his bicycle; it was buckled. Behind the odd collection of people stood William and Ben; both had their arms folded, and both of them wore self-satisfied grins.

"*Look!*" shouted the lady, thrusting the gnome even closer to Uncle Charlie's face for inspection. "My lovely gnome – ruined!"

Uncle Charlie felt sorry for the lady, but had no idea what the broken garden ornament had to do with him. The man with the damaged flamingo presented his complaint next; his face was bright red with rage.

"And will you just look at *this*!" he thundered.

As for the stranger with the buckled bicycle wheel, he was speechless. He just pointed to the wheel, and to a large bruise that was swelling on his knee. Uncle Charlie was at a loss for words, wondering why these complaints were being aimed at him. He felt he'd slipped into a strange dream where nothing made any sense.

"I'm very sorry," he said at last, "but I've absolutely no idea why you seem to think I'm responsible for any of this. I've been talking to a friend on the 'phone for nearly an hour."

"*Just* as I thought," stated the lady with the gnome. "Irresponsible! While you've been busy chatting, that – *thing* – has wrecked my pond and smashed my lovely gnomes!" She pointed towards her house, and everyone, including Uncle Charlie, turned their heads to look in that direction. Cruising blissfully on the surface of the lady's ornamental pond was the goose.

Ice-cold sweat coursed down Uncle Charlie's back as he watched the creature. All too quickly, he remembered leaving the side gate open when he'd dashed in to answer the telephone. He felt angry with himself for his thoughtlessness. A few unguarded moments had undone the peace that had been carefully restored.

Everyone seemed to be talking at once again, except William and Ben, who continued to stand with fixed grins lighting up their faces, revelling in the drama and in Uncle Charlie's discomfort. The poor man slumped down on the doorstep; he wasn't sure whether to laugh or cry. When he looked at the goose, he had a strong desire to laugh out loud. Who could blame the creature? Water: a whole pool of it, available for bathing on a warm day. Uncle Charlie reflected how the carelessness of someone out fishing for the day had forced the wild goose to live so close to humans. How was it supposed to distinguish between water meant for geese, and the forbidden water of an ornamental pond?

The goose had slipped easily through to the front garden while Uncle Charlie had been distracted by the telephone. How pleased he had been to find a big pond; so nearby, too. The green and weedy water had beckoned to him. Keen to feel it beneath his body, he had pushed his way through the assortment of painted plaster gnomes arranged around the pond, knocking them over like skittles. They broke very easily. The gnomes had displayed a variety of poses: some lay on their sides; some read books; one sat fishing. Having waddled, splashed, preened himself and swum for a while, the goose had suddenly spied the plastic flamingo bent stiffly over a patch of shrubs in the next garden.

Perhaps memories of the vicious swan at the sanctuary had flashed before him, and the sight of the long, white, swan-like neck of the flamingo had fuelled his attack upon the ornament. Spitting, hissing and honking loudly, the goose had knocked it off balance and torn into its beak. At this point, the object's owner had appeared at the window to investigate the source of the disturbance. To his horror, he had witnessed the downfall of his flamingo. Opening his front door, he'd rushed screaming and shouting towards the goose, who'd fled back to the pond to cool off. The man had tried without success to chase the goose out of the water, armed with a broom. Unfortunately, a passing cyclist had appeared on the scene and, distracted by the incident, had swerved and hit the kerb, buckling his wheel. The sudden collision had sent him flying over the handlebars and on to the verge.

Uncle Charlie had no defence. The goose seemed to sense his friend's sadness. Obediently he followed Uncle Charlie from the pond back to the house. The group of people on Uncle Charlie's doorstep hastily huddled together as the goose was led past. Uncle Charlie didn't speak to the goose; he just led him to the den and locked the door.

Offering apologies, the poor man sat down in his front room to write out cheques to pay for the damages, just as he had been obliged to do for William and Ben. Uncle Charlie realized that the money returned from the ransom was now paying for the cost of all the breakages. As each person received their cheque, they expressed the opinion that Uncle Charlie hadn't heard the last of the matter. Once again, the words "THE GOOSE HAS TO GO!" rang in his ears.

Chapter 22

Uncle Charlie peered through his curtains at a little group of neighbours congregating around the lady with the pond. He considered for a moment, that her gnomes were made of plaster and, like the man's flamingo, were produced in a factory where they were manufactured in their thousands. When these people had been confronted by a living, breathing creature, they had shunned it and tried to banish it from their neat, orderly little lives and gardens. Didn't they realize the goose had survived an awful ordeal? He had returned safe and alive! The thought of their petty-mindedness saddened him, but as he stood watching the woman picking up the pieces of her broken ornaments and trampled pot plants, which she obviously cherished, he began to feel very sorry for her. He knew what had happened was wrong, and realized he couldn't expect everyone to feel the same way about the goose as he or his nephew felt. When he appeared at the lady's side to offer help, she politely, but curtly, refused him. He apologized again and promised that he would find a new home for the goose, just as soon as possible.

Josh hadn't appeared after school that day. A school football match, played away, meant it would have been too late for him to visit his uncle's house. When Uncle Charlie picked up the telephone to hear his nephew's voice, enquiring about the goose, he was lost for words. Taking a deep breath, he related the events of the morning, ending by saying they needed to meet the next day to discuss the goose's future.

"It's no good!" Uncle Charlie sighed, not long after Josh's arrival the next day. "We *must* face the fact that my home isn't the perfect environment for a goose. I admit he's happy, but he needs more space and freedom, and we can't risk another mishap." He ran his hand over his forehead. "If we don't find somewhere of *our* choice for him soon, then the *neighbours* will ensure he's removed by some sort of authority – goodness only knows where he'd end up. They have the *right* to do that, Josh."

"*Horrible lot!*" seethed Josh. "They were buzzing around like flies when the newspapers and television were interested. Where are they now? Ganging up together to get rid of him!" Josh was miserable and very angry. "After everything he's been through, too!" He banged his fist on the table.

Uncle Charlie looked down at the goose, who was sitting quietly in a box in the corner of the kitchen. He reached for a long list of people who had telephoned, or written, to say they would be happy to take the poor creature if, at any time, Uncle Charlie could no longer keep him. Beside each name, he had made a few notes. He looked down the list.

"Listen, Josh. There are some very kind people here who took the trouble to contact me. Lots of them seem worth investigating to see whether they would be suitable to care for him. There's even one family who lives close by on a farm; we could pay regular visits! They've got a girl about your age." Uncle Charlie smiled, hoping his nephew would be pleased.

"*Great!*" grumbled Josh sarcastically, "Just what I need to hear: some soppy girl wants to care for him! She'd probably try to put bows in his feathers." Josh looked at his uncle, and instantly regretted his words. "I'm sorry, Uncle Charlie. I've been so unkind to you; I realize you're trying to help, but I just *know* he won't stay with anyone else – we're like a family to him, now."

A series of sharp rings on the doorbell made Uncle Charlie jump out of his chair. William stood on the doorstep, ready to fire a question:

"*Well!* When's *it* going, then? If it sets one foot near my leeks, there'll be *trouble!*" he threatened.

Uncle Charlie showed incredible self-control in talking to William. He assured him that the matter was being dealt with urgently, realizing, as he looked at the man, just how much he disliked living between the two petty-minded gardeners. He doubted they would ever move, and the thought of his retirement years, spent sandwiched between them, depressed him.

Josh sat in silence while Uncle Charlie drove him home that evening. Before he got out, he told his uncle to go ahead and contact the person on the list most likely to provide a good home for the goose. Uncle Charlie promised he would do his best. He watched Josh slouch off down the path to his front door and knew there was no way of consoling the boy. Now, he turned to the job of finding the goose a new place to live. He knew the task had to be done as soon as possible.

Chapter 23

The voices at the other end of the telephone all seemed to be genuinely concerned for the welfare of the goose. Uncle Charlie rang his way down the list, making even more detailed notes. By the end of the day, he'd managed to reach most of the people. Some had splendid living conditions to offer a goose, others had lots of experience in keeping them.

Uncle Charlie felt more confused than ever. He rested from the task for half an hour, then considered the list again. He found himself returning to one name in particular. She was a very elderly lady who lived alone. She had cared for lots of injured birds over the years, and kept a few old geese and ducks which had been brought to her with injuries. She'd cared well for them. They had all the freedom they needed on her land. She wasn't at all fussy about her home: her feathered friends were welcomed both inside and out; they came first in her life. Her son had dug a large pond, keeping its setting natural by planting reeds and creating a muddy waddling area. Uncle Charlie decided the goose should go to her.

Arrangements were made for the elderly lady to give the goose a trial period at her home. Uncle Charlie told Josh of his decision, and invited him to help take the goose over to her. He could think of no way to make Josh's parting from the goose any easier, so he tried to involve him. Josh declined to go; he couldn't bear to take the goose to yet another new home.

The day the goose was due to leave, Josh arrived early to spend some time with him. Uncle Charlie packed some necessary items in the back of the van, while Josh sat and stroked the goose's head, promising himself that he would never attempt to see him again.

Josh felt it would be better that way, if the lady was to stand the chance of forming a good relationship with the goose. Josh took one last look at him and said goodbye, before Uncle Charlie drove him away in the van.

Chapter 24

No one was more surprised than Uncle Charlie to hear from the elderly lady, only a week after delivering the goose to her, that he had taken very well to his new home. He'd shown no inclination to leave. Uncle Charlie was delighted; he had a feeling that the dear old lady would win the goose's affection. Josh received the news with mixed feelings. He was pleased the goose had settled so quickly, but saddened to think he had forgotten him and Uncle Charlie so soon. Deep down, he still felt close to the goose, and was finding it hard to reconcile himself to the fact that the creature had really gone this time.

Another week elapsed, and the lady contacted Uncle Charlie again. She reported that the goose was still faring well and showing himself to be a creature of habit. Every morning he would feed and preen himself before wandering down to the front gate, where he sat and watched out for any passers-by. She was amused that he spent time by the gate in the afternoons, too, as well as the evenings.

The telephone rang one afternoon, just as Uncle Charlie had sunk his spade into the earth on his allotment. He was hoping it would be Josh; it was time he took the boy fishing again. Josh hadn't been to visit since the goose had gone. Uncle Charlie was surprised to find it wasn't his nephew, but the elderly lady once again. She sounded slightly anxious. The goose was well and still hadn't made any attempt to leave, but she was concerned about the frequency of his visits to the front gate. Over the past week, they had increased to the point where he was spending most of his days sitting there. She felt it was as though he was waiting for something – or someone. She was also worried that he had taken to missing his morning feed in order to get to the gate earlier. If anyone approached, he would become quite excited, until they had passed. Patiently, he would then resume his vigil. It distressed her to see him, just waiting.

It didn't take Uncle Charlie long to realize what was happening. It was as clear as daylight to him that the goose felt his stay with the lady was only temporary. He was waiting for the return of his friends to take him home again. Uncle Charlie was lost; he couldn't even turn to Josh. It was obvious the boy was pining for the goose as much as the creature was missing him. Turning the problem over in his mind, Uncle Charlie wandered into the garden for some fresh air. There was no denying it, the goose was very homesick. He was showing his feelings more eloquently than any words by waiting, in hope, for them to come for him. And then there was the elderly lady; it wasn't fair that she should need to feel anxious. Uncle Charlie would have to find yet another solution – immediately!

"How's that *goose*?" Ben's mocking voice rose from the other side of his fence. "No doubt it's causing havoc somewhere else these days." He was spraying his garden flowers with something foul-smelling. Uncle Charlie lifted his head to look over the fence and give Ben a piercing stare. When it lasted for over a minute, Ben appeared to be very uncomfortable; he shuffled awkwardly on the spot.

"All right, are you?" ventured Ben, nervously. He was disturbed by his neighbour's strange, fixed expression.

But an idea had suddenly taken root in Uncle Charlie's mind, and was forming itself into the solution to an extremely urgent problem. As he returned from his daydream, a twinkle appeared in his eyes. The corners of his mouth began to turn upwards, too, in an impish grin. When his face had broadened into a huge smile, he announced:

"Yes, Ben! I *am* all right – very all right, since you ask. *And* very grateful to you, too! You've just helped me find the answer to all my problems, and possibly changed my life – for the better! If you and William hadn't been such *dreadful* neighbours, I might never have had such a wonderful idea."

Ben's mouth fell open in disbelief, as he watched Uncle Charlie leap up and punch the air like a striker who's just scored a goal. He ran back into the house. Several minutes later, he'd left in his van, on urgent business in the centre of town.

Chapter 25

Josh received a message at school informing him that his Uncle Charlie would be collecting him that day. A week had elapsed since Uncle Charlie had run excitedly from the garden, leaving Ben in a state of complete bewilderment.

Josh knew nothing of the incident and felt sure his uncle was picking him up from school to take him fishing. He decided to appear enthusiastic. If he was honest, he really didn't care if he never saw a pond, river or canal bank again; he was still missing the goose. Poor Uncle Charlie, it wasn't his fault the goose had been made to leave – just circumstances beyond even his control.

At the sight of the old van parked outside Josh's school, the boy forced a smile and walked towards his uncle.

"About time we visited some water, Josh. Do you a power of good!" Josh fastened his seat-belt, while Uncle Charlie put the van into first gear, and they thundered off down the road. The boy made an effort to talk by telling his uncle about his day at school. Uncle Charlie could tell, by his nephew's tone of voice, that Josh was only trying to be polite. The journey came to an abrupt end when Uncle Charlie swept the van into a car park near to where they had fished on the canal many times. As they got out of the van, Uncle Charlie spoke with enthusiasm.

"There's something I'd like to show you, Josh."

His nephew frowned. He was puzzled by his uncle's remark, especially since he'd noticed there was no fishing gear in the van. But, obediently, he followed Uncle Charlie to the canal towpath. In front of them were moored a cluster of brightly-painted canal boats. They walked towards them. Josh crashed into his uncle, when the man came to a sudden halt in front of a canal boat, which smelled of fresh paint. Confused, Josh looked at the gleaming paintwork, and then at his Uncle Charlie. The man wore a mysterious smile.

"Come on. Follow me!" he said.

Josh couldn't understand; his uncle was walking up the gangplank. With both feet firmly planted on the boat, Uncle Charlie turned and, opening wide his arms, announced, "Welcome to my new home, Josh!"

Josh stared in disbelief.

"Come on! It's for *real*." Uncle Charlie beckoned excitedly. "Let's go in. I'll be sharing it with a friend; I'd like you to meet him."

Chapter 26

Uncle Charlie led Josh down the steps to the living quarters. The next few moments made the boy feel as though he was part of someone else's dream. Inside, the canal boat shone with highly-polished wood and gleaming brass fittings. Josh passed through the little kitchen and the living room; everywhere was colourfully decorated. A door near the end of the boat led to the sleeping quarters. As Uncle Charlie began to open it, Josh heard a familiar sound coming from the other side.

"AARGH-HONK! AARGH-HONK!" The goose burst through the door in his enthusiasm to get to Josh, almost knocking him over.

Josh sat down to recover from the shock of his uncle's amazing announcement. Over a cup of tea, Uncle Charlie carefully explained the events of the last week that had led to them sitting in his new, floating home. Josh stroked the goose's head as he heard how the elderly lady who'd taken the goose had become worried when he'd spent most of his days by the gate, waiting for something, or someone.

Uncle Charlie described how he'd wrestled with the problem of the goose when, suddenly, inspiration had come from a most unlikely source: his neighbour, Ben. He had realized it would be impossible to bring the goose back home again, but there was nothing to stop him from moving away, and taking the goose along with him. He didn't need to live next to William or Ben! He could leave the awful, grumbling gardeners: go anywhere, and live anywhere! He was as free as a bird – a goose, to be exact. And, as they both loved water, for different reasons, only one place would really suit them. Uncle Charlie had always longed for one of the canal boats. He had recalled seeing one for sale, and dashed to make an offer. He had put his house on the market, at a very low price, and was delighted to find it snapped up almost immediately. On the day he moved in, he had collected the goose from the elderly lady. She had been so pleased he was to be reunited with the two people he now, so obviously, considered to be his family.

Josh sat wide-eyed as he listened to his uncle tell of his plans to use the boat for pleasure trips in the future. He'd even considered fishing trips, but remembered the goose. That was one creature who didn't need to be near a fishing-line ever again, if it could be avoided. Josh smiled happily to himself as he stroked the goose. The boy's head was in a spin. Uncle Charlie would take him home that evening, but ahead of him stretched long summer days, to be spent on the canal boat with his uncle and the remarkable goose.

They spent a while outside watching the goose swimming on the canal. He was as inquisitive as ever. Fish darted beneath him, ducks swam around him, and high above the familiar cry of two geese could be heard. He was content. Uncle Charlie's inspiration had solved all their problems. Now the goose was able to enjoy the water as well as the companionship of the two creatures he wanted most of all in his life. He was free to come and go as he pleased – they would always be there for him.

Uncle Charlie waved to a friendly new neighbour, living on another canal boat, as he and Josh walked down the gangplank. Josh was still half-expecting to wake up from a dream. He turned to look back at the canal boat and noticed that his uncle had started to letter a name for it in yellow and gold paint on its side. With great skill, he had completed the first three letters; the rest were pencilled in. Josh peered closer so that he could read them. He spoke the words quietly to himself. There really could be no better name for his uncle's boat: "GOOSE ON THE RUN".

Midnight Dancer

Elizabeth Lindsay

Ride into adventure with Mory and her pony,
Midnight Dancer

Book 1: Midnight Dancer
Mory is thrilled when she finds the perfect pony.
But will she be allowed to keep her?

Book 2: Midnight Dancer: To Catch a Thief
There's a thief with his eye on Mory's mother's sapphire
necklace – and it's down to Mory and Midnight Dancer
to save the day...

Book 3: Midnight Dancer: Running Free
Mory and Dancer have a competition to win. But they
also have a mystery to solve...

Book 4: Midnight Dancer: Fireraisers
There's trouble on Uncle Glyn's farm – because there's
a camper who loves playing with fire. Can Mory and
Dancer avert disaster?

Book 5: Midnight Dancer: Joyriders
Mory's rival, Caroline, has her twin cousins to stay.
And they look like trouble. . .

Book 6: Midnight Dancer: Ride By Night
Sheep are disappearing from the hillsides, and Mory
and Midnight Dancer are determined to help. . .

HiPPO ANiMAL

Have you ever longed for a puppy to love, or a horse of your own? Have you ever wondered what it would be like to make friends with a wild animal? If so, then you're sure to fall in love with these fantastic titles from Hippo Animal!

Thunderfoot
Deborah van der Beek
When Mel finds the enormous, neglected horse Thunderfoot, she doesn't know it will change her life for ever...

Vanilla Fudge
Deborah van der Beek
When Lizzie and Hannah fall in love with the same dog, neither of them will give up without a fight...

A Foxcub Named Freedom
Brenda Jobling
An injured vixen nudges her young son away from her. She can sense danger and cares nothing for herself – only for her son's freedom...